STORIES LC

STORIES LONG SHORT & TALL

Best Wishes

Contents

Dedication 2

Acknowledgements 3

The Navigator 4

Tickling Fish 24

Paul's Story... 27

My Writing Workshop 33

Sleep Dreams 34

Not Lost... 38

Creative Thoughts 42

Granny's Soundbox.. 45

The first time I saw a dragon 51

Petit's Pawnshop (1901-1968) 56

Daniel Gerrick's VR Quest 86

Ugthorpe Mill (A Family of Millers) 95

The Travel Chest 99

The Clockmaker.. 102

Just a Thought 105

The Ghost.. 122

The Mystery of Ebbe House 131

The Man Behind the Nab (With the rhubarb slippers) 154

It's all in the Attic (You can always change your mind).......... 157

The Old Writing Desk 163

Chasing Rainbows.. 166

About the Author 170

Other books by John... 172

Acknowledgements

My youngest grandson, Jules, who joined with me in writing 'The first time I saw a dragon.'
JV Author Services, to whom I entrusted editing and final formatting.

Cover image designed by Freepik.

The Navigator

We tend to believe what we see and hear and then create a story around it. A story of how things seem and then become how things are. This is the same for all of us. At eighteen, James had experienced a loving family and joy in his emerging years, followed by tragedy and confusion as to what comes next.

Morning Run – It was a Saturday morning in Whitby. Dark clouds filled the sky, and there was a bit of a breeze, but the weather would not deter him. James had his routine and would stick to it regardless.

His mom, Elizabeth, called from her room. "James, is that you?"

"Yes, Mom, I'm just off for my run. See you later."

"Okay, stay safe," she called.

It's doubtful he heard the last bit as he closed the door behind him and immediately broke into a slow jog. The large stone steps rose before him, out of Blackburn's Yard and towards the Abbey. Saturday mornings were special, with a sense of holiday and a distinct set of sounds echoing through the streets. Whatever the weather, he was out running, his feet hammering the earth along the Cleveland Way.

James Ward was now eighteen, and running gave him a sense of freedom. The wind – with him or against him drove him onwards. Today, the wind was off the land and gusting quite strongly. Reaching the Abbey, he knew he was not out to break any records but to enjoy the run. He rested at Ling Hill, stared at the lighthouse, and took several long breaths. He was unaware of how dangerously close he was to the edge of the cliff when suddenly, a gust of wind almost took him off his feet. James instinctively threw himself to the ground. Adrenaline raced through his veins as thoughts flashed through his mind. What if he had fallen? What would it feel like to fall from such a height – would he be dead before he hit the rocks below? Fear, it seems, exists only when anticipating a future outcome. Today, James' fear arose as an attachment to a past episode, though he was not consciously aware at that moment.

All was well, and that's all that mattered. He quickly returned to his feet as seagulls high above were skilfully navigating the wind. Deciding he had run far enough that morning, he set off homeward at a slow pace. A side wind shifted slightly, pushing him forward as his pace increased. He was a competitive young man and a member of the local Harriers, although running on his own would be his preference. The pounding became hypnotic as James had the

Abbey in his sights – the finishing line. Suddenly, a roar came from behind him, and he glanced over his shoulder. "Wardy, Wardy, too slow to catch cold," Marty shouted as he and two others raced past. One day, James said to himself. But not today. Let them have their fun. Marty (Martin Fletcher) had always been the one to make snide remarks ever since junior school. Whitby is the kind of town where everyone knows everyone and most of their history, too. Trust him to be a member of the Harriers. "One day, Marty," he muttered as he slowed to a steady jog.

Coming up to the Abbey, there was no one in sight. He burst into a full-on sprint, visualising a finishing line some two hundred metres ahead. He wanted to know if the speed was there when he needed it. Breaking through the imaginary winning tape, his legs carried him on to a slow stop. The sound of his heart beating loudly in his head, chest heaving, and every breath felt like a sharp knife. The sweat from his shirt felt cool in the breeze and he took a satisfying, long intake of breath.

James' route home from the Abbey was down the steep cobbled lane known as Donkey Path. There was a snicket leading off to the left and along to the top of their yard. There was always something new to see among the maze of Whitby rooftops, a town divided by the harbour with its dwindling fishing fleet. The sight held him for a moment as he paused there above their yard. Then, descending the stone steps like a mountain goat, he was home safe.

Parcel Post – There was a parcel waiting for him

on the kitchen table. Mom, standing with her arms folded, nodded towards the neat package. "This came with the postman this morning."

Puzzled, James looked closely at the markings as he turned the package over in his hands. Knowing that the only way to find out what was inside was to open it,

Mother watched with curiosity. "It's not even close to your birthday, and I don't recognise the handwriting. And another thing, we don't know anyone from Norfolk."

The mystery was not that they had no idea where the package was from or who had sent it. The address label was clear. The parcel was for James Ward. The wrapping paper revealed a sealed inner parcel.

Mother continued, "Wasn't there another James Ward at your old school? Such a common name in these parts. Perhaps you shouldn't open it."

It was too late for that. Anyway, it was the correct address, and finally, the contents were visible – an impressive old book embossed with the title 'Navigation.' Even the book itself was tied with string, finishing with a double bow. Somehow, it felt heavier than the original package. James noticed the Compass Rose symbol and sensed this was a book of immense value. "It looks like a book that Dad would have liked, maybe not for a teenager, though. So, why is it here? Why me?" He took the packaging to bits piece by piece, but there was no letter or message of any kind that would throw light on who had sent it or, more importantly, why. Often, there's a small label on the outer packaging, showing the sender's details – but no.

James' father had died three years and two days ago. He and Mom had visited the cemetery up on Larpool Lane just the other day. They laid flowers by the headstone and spoke to him as if he were there with them. James pondered on his father's old saying: 'When you're gone, you're gone – not in the ground, that's just your body.' Also, he would say, 'There are more adventures beyond this life, of which I am certain.' James was still very bitter about the fact that his dad (Andy) had left them. He knew there was no choice in the matter – accidents happen. Andy lived for walking and would have loved to have gone on an expedition to some far-off land. However, that was not to happen. He was content to discover paths he had never walked before here in his beloved home county of North Yorkshire.

It was a day like any other. Andy packed some supplies and off he went in the car across to the Yorkshire Dales. It was unusual as there had been no contact, and when he didn't return home, alarms were sent out, and the mountain rescue team found his body. They will never know if it was a trip, a slip, or what he was doing before his fall. He was always so careful – it didn't make sense. The rescue team said there wasn't a mark on him. It was as if he were sleeping.

Mom straightened out the wrapping paper and looked once more before throwing it in the bin. The book remained tied and on the kitchen table. A strange feeling went through her, a memory of a double bow somewhere in the past. "Breakfast is almost ready, enough time for you to wash. Come on, off you go." Her words were still aimed at a seven-year-old. James just smiled and said he would only be two minutes. Mom laid out the cutlery and moved the book onto the window ledge and soon they were sitting, enjoying eggs, beans and sausage. It was a little surprising that when James reached for the book, his mom didn't tell him off. I am sure she was as keen to see more about the book as he was. The knot was quite tight, so he cut through the string with a pair of scissors without hesitation, preserving the double bow.

"Is there anything written on the inside cover," Mom asked, "such as this book belongs to?"

"No, nothing here. But notes are scribbled on most pages, and parts of the text have been underlined."

"Well, what does it say? There must be some clues as to who wrote it."

"It's not easy to read. As I said, it's scribbled. I'll have to give it time and study it."

"Give it here. Let me try." She reached for her glasses and took a drink of water before resting the open book on the edge of the table. "I see what you mean. It looks like a spider has crawled across the page. Is this one of your friends having a joke?"

"An expensive one if you look at the cost of postage, and why go to the trouble of writing all these words? I'm just going to have to read it cover to cover. It looks interesting, though."

Later that evening, James ran an errand to the local shop and completed some college notes. Mom had music playing in the background while she finished the ironing, and James came into the kitchen. "I'm going on up to bed, an early night. I'm having a hot chocolate, do you want one? I thought I would read a few pages of this book."

Her focus remained on the ironing. "No, I'm fine, thanks." Another shirt was folded. "I still have a strange feeling about that book. Perhaps you should give it to the charity shop."

"I'll see." A term his mother used when, really, she meant no. James picked up his drink and went up the two flights of stairs to his bedroom in the attic. Streetlights reflected the colours of the rooftops across the town as he closed the curtains. Sitting upright with covers around him, Navigation was resting against his bent knees. The first task, he thought, would be to scan through the pages and see if he could pick up any clues as to its origin. No hints were apparent. He soon realised that although this was a nautical textbook, the annotations were pointing more to a journey of self-discovery. This was an opportune time in his life to discover who he was and where he was going – although that thought was not consciously clear to him. Sleep was going to get the better of him that night, but Sunday would be a free day for him to continue reading.

Lazy Sunday – James stirred from his slumber to the sound of church bells. He was tempted to roll over and go back to sleep, but the seagulls added to the din.

Then there's Mom calling up the stairs. "I'm off to church in ten minutes, still time for you to come?"

The reply was more of a grunt, and Mom

decided not to push it. There was a time when all three of them went to church each Sunday. James seemed happy there and mixed well with the other children. But things changed, especially when they lost Andy, a loving husband and father. The notion of family had been missing, and both mother and son were still in grief.

The house fell quiet, and James climbed back into bed with a cup of tea and a biscuit, with the book opened against his knees. He needed to identify the secondary author. Without evidence, he decided to call him the Navigator. It helped to visualise someone about the same size and build as Andy, who also had lots of experience with maps and a compass. On the first page, in blue ink, were the words, 'To navigate is simply to find your way around and know where you are.' This could certainly have been written by Andy, though his writing was much neater than this. James had often imagined that his father had not died but just gone away and would return one day. The book created an emotional link that had been missing, and he read on with interest. The church bells, seagulls and other sounds seemed to disappear the more he became absorbed in the book. James needed a plan, a way to pick through the data and begin to make sense of it. He jumped out of bed and rummaged through his top drawer. A yellow highlighter was not his favourite colour, but it would help things stand out as he marked significant parts.

The text of the book begins with the insistence on preparation, setting out on a journey with all the necessary gadgets: maps, compass, sextant, the list went on – Items for plotting a course using the sun and the stars by night. Andy would have taken a whistle, torch, and mobile phone – how did he not call for help? Was his death instant? By now, James was getting used to deciphering the scribble. References, such as making plans first and checking that all the bases are covered (the what-ifs in life). Part of James could see the sense in this, but the time it would take… surely it is quicker to just get on with the task? The words: Don't be put off, superstition is rife among sailors and many of us… caused him to stop. Superstition is when we create a story because we don't understand something, James added: Learn to distinguish the truth. When you are at sea, there is nothing around you but water.

James knew there was a truth and a purpose to this book. It had to have something to do with his father, for there were many similarities, or was this just wishful thinking? Memories were flooding back of Dad's wise words and phrases; he was always prepared for anything, and no matter what he was doing, everything was set out like a military operation. This was now something missing around the house. As James became more engrossed in the content of the book, the need to discover who and why the book was sent to him faded.

Plan the Route – The book and the highlighter went under the bed as James felt the need for a bowl of cereal. Putting on yesterday's clothes, he ran downstairs, hair still tousled, and teeth not brushed – he would shower when he got back. There was a plan emerging that involved a walk from the Abbey to the lighthouse. This would soon be a race, a round trip and a total of just over four miles. There was already a buzz about this at the Harriers club – another group from Scarborough were also entering.

He dropped the empty cereal bowl into the sink and threw some items into a small backpack – a rain Mac, a mobile phone, a couple of oranges and a bar of dark chocolate. He found a small notepad and a pencil and wrote a message to his mom. 'Gone for a recon walk to the lighthouse. See you later. J x.' The notepad and pencil were dropped into his side pocket. This was an important mission to plot the route and note the pitfalls. This is a beautiful route along the cliff tops, however, there are rugged parts. All races are serious, and this would be a new approach. James felt he was putting into practice what he had learned from the Navigator. The more he knew each footstep of the way, the more he could focus on winning the race. The date had been set, less than three weeks away. Already, there had been snide remarks from Marty – why did he have to be so mean? If James could beat him fair and square, perhaps that would be the end of it.

Once James had started the route, he opted to use his phone camera to store images of the path with its dips and turns, places to pick up speed and where to conserve energy. These notes he chose to store again on his phone's voice recorder – this was much easier, and he felt like a professional. The motivation to win had never been higher, and self-belief seemed to have increased ten-fold as James could see himself lifting the trophy high above his head. Doubt crept in as James recalled the last time that they were up against Scarborough, they had some decent runners, though Marty was the one to beat. This was a great project, though the time went swiftly by. James documented each part of the track, changes in surface and much more.

Arriving home, he greeted his mom and looked around for something to eat.

"There's no filling you some days," she said. "There will be food on the table in just under the hour. Are there any pots in your bedroom that need to come down?"

"No, it was all cleared this morning before I left. I'll just go and put these in my room and change my shirt. How was church?"

James didn't wait for an answer and Mom just said it was fine. They were never a family for strict Sunday lunches, as Andy was often away at weekends. Mom had prepared a stew in the slow cooker, which smelled awesome.

The conversation over late lunch seemed different; James picked up more than usual and listened to his mom's emotional side. He did feel this was a little unusual, though pleasant. Even after they'd eaten, he offered to wash up and then retrieved his phone notes from upstairs and settled into the armchair.

Mom had relaxed on her part of the sofa with her book. "You not going to your room?"

"No, I thought I'd sit here with you. Are you okay with me keeping my headphones on? I'm going over the recordings of the track?"

Mom replied with a simple, that's nice. The pair enjoyed the closeness, and time passed by quietly, with James pondering his route and living every step.

Confrontation – A proposal was passed. The Harriers would meet at The Black Swan on Baxtergate the following Wednesday. James couldn't understand why a business meeting should be mixed with a social event. For James, there was never such a thing as a simple night out, which is probably why he avoided them. Marty was sure to be there. So, plan B was to avoid him – opposite sides of the room seemed preferable. At that stage, there was no plan C.

The evening convened with a pep talk about the coming race from their respected leader, who was in the habit of harking back to his days as cross-country champion. He was a little older than James' dad but had a very similar background. A third-generation fisherman with a larger coble and forward wheelhouse moored by the South wall of the inner dock. By now, formalities and words of encouragement were out of the way, and a group of lads descended upon the bar. Marty was already on his third pint by James' reckoning and flexing his perceived authority – no one was going to challenge him.

Though he had his back towards James, the next comment was clearly addressed to him. "Lonely boy is not a team player and will never achieve anything."

James' inner voice advocated that no response was his best option. Another part of him wanted to take a full swing at his smug face. The unknown plan C kicked in, and James downed his drink and left by the front door. Teamwork: A ship and its navigation rely on well-practised routines. Charts are drawn by seafarers who have been there. James had also grasped the meaning of the word accountability. Marty, however, manipulated everyone.

Moments later, a voice behind him. "Wait up, James, he didn't mean that." It was Mike, the peacemaker – this was not going to work.

James shouted, "Martin Fletcher has gone too far. I am done with him. This will be sorted on the track."

Mike tried again. "We do have to be a team, especially against the Scarborough lot."

"Teamwork, Mike, comes out of respect. Marty has no respect for anyone but himself. I recognise now that the only things I can change are the things within me. I'm sick of his petty words and putting me down. There is a new me coming, and he'd better look out." Over twelve years of bowing down to Marty came spilling out on the street – and it was not over yet, not by a long way. James was beginning to make internal changes. Choosing to change the things that were his to do – letting go of other people's stuff – and it felt good. Was this the real James that seemed to have been hiding for so long? He knew in the core of his being that this was right, not as a fight but as a way to assert his rightful position. Marty could make of it what he will – that would be his problem. This was about holding fast when things get tough – managing fear and other emotions. Trim the sails and hold the course – lessons from the Navigator. Mike turned back to join the group as James walked towards the swing bridge and home. He felt lighter and much taller – the race was on, and the stakes were high.

The Navigator – One week before the race,

James was out running, and as he approached Ling Hill, he caught sight of a figure sitting with his back against the lighthouse wall. Drawing closer, the man stood and looked his way.

James was within ten metres as the man shouted, "Go on, lad, you can do it." He had a great beam on his face, and his voice came from deep inside. James felt compelled to stop and frowned at the man who was neatly dressed in tweeds – not what you expect on the Cleveland Way. "Don't stop on my account," the man said. "You have work to do."

"Do I know you?" James said. "Are you from Scarborough?"

"No, on both accounts."

James came a little closer – there was something familiar – and he felt quite safe in his presence. The man had a weathered yet kindly face, and James thought he may be younger than he looked, even in his early forties (around his dad's age).

His next question floored James. "You will be James Ward?"

James was caught off guard. "How do you know me, and who are you?" James had his new voice, more assertive and in control – there were things he needed to know.

"Well, my guess is you might call me the Navigator." There was a stunned silence as the man realised that James had received the book he had sent him. James was busy trying to think of his next question, of which there were many. The Navigator continued. "I am sorry for interrupting your run. You look very determined. This was not a planned meeting. I am spending a couple of days out at Hawsker and decided to come out for a walk. This is purely a chance meeting. However, I am curious to know how you are getting on with the book?"

James smiled. "Well, it's an interesting book and I am learning much more about life than putting out to sea. There are such things as Sea Monsters and coping with the unexpected. You have a local accent, but do you live in Norfolk?"

The Navigator chuckled. "Oh no, I live in Middlesbrough – but posted it while on business in Norfolk. The book was my lifesaver and stayed with me. It was while I was there I decided to send it to you. I thought it might help a young lad growing up."

James was determined to know more about this mystery man, who seemed to know a lot about him. "So, what's the connection – how do you know me? You must have a proper name?" Inside, James was shaking, awaiting the answer to so many things.

"You're right, young man. I have not been completely honest with you. I have my reasons. I'll try and keep it short. My name is Greg Smithson, and I was a good friend of your dad's. I was also best man at his wedding to your lovely mother, Elizabeth."

James had been right to see traits of his dad in the book notes.

"We split up big time," Greg continued. "It was my fault. Work was good, and money a plenty, but drink was my downfall. Your dad tried to help, but I pushed him away and said some awful things to them both."

"Why did you not come back when Dad

died?" James could see the pain on Greg's face.

"I was still in a bad place, though I was there in the graveyard. Nobody saw me. It's only in the last two years that I have pulled my life around, with the help of Alcoholics Anonymous and the Navigation book."

James could make clearer sense of the book's handwriting now. "How did you find the book?"

Greg paused, then replied, "I think the book found me. I stumbled across it in a charity shop. I was only there to get warm and tried to look intent on buying. There was no resistance. The book seemed to fly into my hands. I just knew it held immense value and was a treasure to behold. The price was one pound, not even enough to buy a coffee, and I had to have it. I remember pulling out a pile of pennies and some silver and laying it on the counter. Just two weeks into an Alcoholics Anonymous recovery programme, I felt the book would be a great distraction during lonely nights in the bedsit. It turned out to be my lifesaver." Greg had been holding close eye contact with James. "I can see your dad in you. I have often thought about you and your mother and how I let you down. I wanted you to have the book to see how helpful it can be. I am back to my old self, the better part of me – it's all work in progress."

Wow, thought James. That was quite a testimony, and he was ready to welcome Greg back into his family. Greg insisted he was not ready for that and was going back to Middlesbrough that same day. "I will catch up with you again soon. You can tell me more about what you found in the book. Run fast, young man. You are still not aware of who you can become and what you will achieve." With that, Greg turned and headed back towards Hawsker. James, with renewed energy and purpose, broke into a smooth run back to the Abbey. The rehearsed path felt like an old friend, and they worked so well together. In his head, James subtracted the time spent with Greg and was pleased with his runtime. He would have loved to tell someone, especially his mom, about the chance meeting with the Navigator. He knew, of course, that this could not happen yet – it would happen when things were right, like today for James.

The Race – Race day finally arrived. There were team strategies set to keep the Scarborough club in their place. James was content to play along with this game, though his personal goal was to win, or at least, he had to beat Marty. James realised that aggression would not bring success. This had to come from a place of confidence and peace of mind. He had already been working on this, together with his physical endurance. A modest four miles was not the toughest of runs but should not be underestimated. James was building a new vision of the world and its characters. This was to be the run of his life.

Assembling at the Abbey car park, nerves were building, but James had his under control. His mind, like a sea captain, reviewing the charts and weather conditions – all eventualities were brought to the table and rested. The strange thing was Marty was out of James' space. Perhaps he had nerves, too? The pre-runs, images and recordings had set the route in his mind – all that was to happen now was to run.

The contestants were brought to the starting line, where the organisers said a few words (that not one of the runners listened to), and they were all keyed up for the gunshot. James glanced briefly to see his mom smile and mouth the words – give it your best son. Finally, the specified firearm dispensed a loud crack that echoed around the ruined abbey walls. There was a rush to go, initially at a higher speed than the runners would have liked. This seemed to be dictated by the Scarborough team. They clearly had a strategy that Whitby had not expected. Stick to your guns, were the words in James' head. There were lengths ahead of them where catch-up could be made. The Whitby team seemed to flounder a little, and it was James who called for a push just four hundred metres on. Two members of the Whitby team followed close to James and guarded his position. His knowledge of the track greatly aided the three of them – a slight lead was occurring. Just over one mile in, the Whitby three were leading the pack by seconds only, and the lighthouse was in sight.

Two marshals ahead marked the turning point. James was shoulder to shoulder with one of his teammates and a challenger from Scarborough. Marty shouted for James to drop back and let him take the lead. James ignored him and trusted his knowledge of the track – he had never felt this strong. Marty began to push his way to the front, the pace had been too strong for many as the group split three or four times. Words from Marty were hurtful and designed to put

James off his mark, but it was as if James had created a bubble around him – nothing was going to get through. Already, he could hear cheers in the distance – the finish line. Was this the moment to break? A force that James had not experienced before coursed through his body and lifted him as he shot forward. Marty tried to hold on just behind, but he slowly fell back. Just twenty or more metres to the line, and James found the time to glance back at Marty, now about eight metres behind with the rest of the group – that look said it all. He really did have the speed when he needed it. The race and much more were his. This was James' day. His teammates congratulated him. 'Great run, lad,' they chorused. The Scarborough team had three in the final group, taking second and third place. Marty, in the end, could only hold onto fourth place – he was beat.

James' mom was there, waving and trying to get to him. He spotted Greg in the crowd and made his way over to him. "I didn't expect to see you today."

"I wouldn't miss it for the world, young man. My, how you've grown."

Mom arrived on the scene with a disapproving remark. "What are you doing here?" She glared at Greg and placed herself between him and her son.

James took her arm and, looking at her, said, "This is not the old Greg. This is the Navigator." James took his mom's hand. "Greg has helped me a lot through the book that saved his life. You need to listen to him. There's a lot you don't know."

Elizabeth remembered the double bow knot.

Greg used it to tie their wedding present, and she and Andy had kept it in a drawer for luck. Timing was everything as James went forward to take his prize. Elizabeth and Greg caught up, and a good amount of healing took place.

Later, they walked together to the Donkey Path, through the snicket and down into Blackburn's Yard. This was an emotional moment for Greg, being welcomed into Andy and Liz's home after so long away.

Tickling Fish

My thoughts turn back to my childhood and a small place on the North York Moors where my mother was born and brought up. Granny's farm, which my uncle and his family then owned, was where I spent many a holiday with my cousins. There was always something to do: collecting eggs, taking the milk cans on, potato picking, hay timing and last thing at night, fastening the hens in. You might imagine it was all work, not a bit, rummaging among the old stuff stored up in the stable chamber, jumping off bails of straw, making dens in the wood, and who would dare go up into the attic and sit in Granny's rocking chair?

Sunday Mass was never to be missed, though what happened after mass was also a ritual. The men folk would gather over the road just to the left of the church gates. The women would form an orderly group just outside the gates, with the girls to their right, and the young boys would be over the road to the left of the men folk. There was a progression for the young lads as they grew in their years. Moving closer towards the men, their conversation moved away from games to farm work, joinery, and such. Within the village, family and friendships were the strongest of bonds and a name carried a lot of weight. There were shared work relationships, a community network spanning distance and time, a sense of belonging and fitting into the way of things.

Now, as kids, we had heard there were trout in the beck, but I can't remember the first time we realised they were big enough to eat. Imagining ourselves as Robinson Crusoe, we talked about how we might catch this tasty wild delight. A rod and a float seemed quite impractical in such a narrow stream, though a net might be a plan. It was one such Sunday morning after mass when one of the older men suggested we tickle the fish with our hands and swish it out and onto the bank side, and we wondered if he was pulling our legs. My uncle was a man to be trusted, and over Sunday lunch, he verified the art, saying that tickling hypnotised the fish so you could grab it.

This newfound practice had to be put to the test, so all seven of us set out down the beck that Sunday afternoon. As we walked beside the running water, our eyes were fixed where we had seen fish before. Talking was reduced to a whisper, and it felt like we were walking on tiptoes. "There," Chris said. "There's one."

I had never known silence like it, just the sound of the rippling stream could be heard. As I approached the edge, I rolled up my sleeves and laid flat face down. The water was cold as I moved my hands slowly toward the undercut bank. My heart skipped two beats as I touched the fish, wiggling my fingers in a tickling motion. The fish seemed quite content as I smiled and nodded to the others. At that moment there was a flash, and he was gone. The disappointing sigh from those who stood around said it all.

We walked for a few hundred yards and came upon a likely spot. The bend in the stream had created an overhanging edge, and there was the biggest fish we had seen. Chris was straight in, and my fingers were twitching. I knew what he was feeling. A moment later, Chris jerked, and it was as if half the stream had come out with the fish. We all got a drenching, but where was the fish? It had to be here among the grass, but it was nowhere to be seen.

Then Bernie, the youngest of the group, frozen to the spot, said, "It's down me wellie." The fish was indeed head first down his wellie, flapping its tail against his bare leg. There was a deed to be done with a stone that was carried out without a word, and the procession back to the farm recounted the excitement repeatedly as we took turns to carry the fish.

There are no fish in these becks today, and the stream is barely a trickle, but the skills and how we learned them became a template for much more than just tickling fish. Remembering the old ways handed down and how often things that seemed improbable/ impossible turn out to be just right.

Paul's Story

Paul, now thirty-five, had lived all his life in Whitby, a place steeped in history, myth, and folklore – it was often difficult to tell one from another. His father had a small fishing boat and brought in a modest income. Something was exciting about the sea, and the young lad would have loved to go out on the boat, but his father always said, 'You are too small, lad. Why, you'd be blown overboard in no time.' Paul spent many hours up on the cliff top, daydreaming as he watched for his father's return.

Paul had a passion for writing. His head was often filled with words, and a figurative dictionary surrounded him. He had the instinct to spell out impressive details about nature and people. Stories were created and then rearranged to suit the situation. All these things seemed to just happen – he had no idea how.

That day, our writer did not intend to spend the afternoon at the picture house, but as the rain came down, he was not the only one heading for cover. The cinema would have been built in the early 1920s and retained a lot of its quirky style – ornate wood panelling, soft carpets, strong springs on the seats, and a prominent smell of popcorn. The building would accommodate up to seven hundred but had not seen a full house in many a year. The lights dimmed, and there was a final shuffle as people settled into their seats. Paul assumed he was just there to kill time and began to relax as the movie started.

The main character was a man in his fifties, beginning in black and white for artistic effect as his early life story was being told. Paul began to take interest as he recognised parallels with his childhood. It was so close that he began to think someone had an insight into his past. Places and even faces were familiar. Terms of phrase echoing from his early life seemed to bellow around the room. Paul had to pinch himself to check he was not asleep. This was all becoming very unnerving, and as the movie became full colour, the hero was the same age as Paul – struggling with who he was and afraid to speak out against adversity. Paul felt the character's fear on a very personal level, born out of his own experiences. It reached the point where the character faced his nemesis, finally refusing to be quiet. Surely, he would become a martyr!

Even though deep down, Paul knew the hero would prevail, he could not stay any longer and opted to leave the cinema. Paul stepped back into the real world. The rain had stopped, though a fair wind was blowing through the streets. There was so much emotion stirring inside him, unresolved fear and frustration – all he wanted to do was walk.

As a writer, it's possible to create the end you want to see, and Paul wondered if he could write a narrative for the hero – for himself. That would be an arduous task while his heart and mind were full of his past failures and discouragement. He needed to separate himself from the movie and his emotions.

Sporadic pedestrians came past him in waves, and his senses became numbed. Then, someone smiling was walking purposely towards him. Paul struggled for recognition and thought it must be for someone behind him.

"Paul. Paul Lawson. Is it you? I haven't seen you since our school days. Brian Taylor – how are you?"

Paul shook the offered hand firmly. "Well, yes, it is, and yes, I remember you. We played on the school basketball team. How are you?"

"I moved back to Whitby this week, and I've been away almost eighteen years. I was just going for a coffee at the Smuggler's Café. How about joining me?"

Paul saw this as a rude interruption to his writing but decided to go along with it. "Yes, okay, but I'm buying. It's good to see you. We had fun times back then, didn't we."

The Smuggler's Café was an old establishment, popular during and before their generation of teens. Paul led the way into the café and pointed. "We'll take those seats by the window. It's table service nowadays."

Brian raised his eyebrows. "The old place still smells the same – rich coffee. But where's the jukebox?"

"Oh, they took that out a while back. It's a little upmarket now. Not the same as when we were kids."

Brian sat while still looking around. "The same cash register. I remember that."

"Pre-decimalisation, it's only for show," Paul said, handing Brian a menu. "What will you have?"

"Got to be a cappuccino, please. This is great, thanks."

In no time at all, the pair had got through the basic summary of where they'd been, what they'd done, family, etc. Brian was in full flow, reminiscing about schoolboy pranks and teachers, that in later years he had valued. Brian insisted on another round of coffee that he would pay for.

Paul had enjoyed his time with his old school pal, though the purpose of his walk had not been fulfilled. Paul hesitated and then said, "Do you remember me when I was young?"

Brian frowned and laughed. "Of course, otherwise I would have walked right past you."

"No. Perhaps I should have said, what do you remember of me? I would like to remember more clearly now – who I was then. That might sound a little crazy?"

Brian gave Paul his full attention. "Not crazy, but a little deep. I would say you were quite ordinary, though you always had your homework in on time. You seemed so organised, so in control. I guess people would say you would go on to do great things."

"That's not how it felt. I was driven by fear of

what would happen if I did not achieve." Had this broken Brian's perception of him? Paul continued. "I didn't mean to kill the conversation. It's just that, years later, you wonder when things stopped – everything seemed fine until…"

"Things changed for me when I moved away."

"Yes. But I don't have that doorway, that point in time – everything stayed the same – though things changed around me, and I'm not the person I was. Even if that was an illusion."

Paul fiddled with his spoon, turning it over and looking at both sides, his image distorted in two ways. As if processing as he spoke, Paul went on. "Strange how we just roll on in life, never checking to see how we are doing or if we are on the right path. Then, one day, we have a reality check, and we wonder how we came this far and who we are." He looked at Brian. "We were good mates, weren't we, and we had some fun. Thanks for that and for listening. It helped a lot. It's been a strange kind of day."

The pair went their separate ways, having exchanged contact numbers. The Smuggler's was to become a frequent meeting place for exchanging memories and future visions.

It was almost a year later, and Paul had dropped into a new normality. Until one day, he found himself in a situation that was none of his business, but he felt compelled to get involved – someone had to speak out. He remembered the movie, which aroused a mixture of emotions, and he knew the risks were high. There was a push forward that was not of his making. Words became clear, though quiet at first, as if only for his ears. Paul's belief in what was right far outweighed his perceived fear. Assuming his full height, Paul's voice boomed out across the room, and all eyes turned towards him.

He had never been so clear, never been so certain in all his life. There was a power in his voice and the words he knew he must say. People began to side with him in support of the truth while at the same time being pressed forward against the aggressors. Paul's heart pounded as he stood firm. Now, with the weight of numbers behind and to the side of him, the opposition had to withdraw. There were cheers and shouts for Paul to take the lead. He was overwhelmed but also felt it was time to step into his new self.

The writer has the power of the word and creates the stories – it's only a small step to use that authority in declaring truth in a way that it can be understood. We are all called to be that voice, perhaps not in the way of Paul's story, but speaking out for the weak and oppressed, relieving suffering, and establishing a better way. So, go and find your voice however you may think it sounds.

STORIES LONG SHORT & TALL

My Writing Workshop

Not a tidy space but order in the chaos,
Fingertip access to detail and thesaurus.
With paper and pens the creator engages,
A wordsmith, bringing life to the pages.

Cushions and covers on an old armchair,
The smell of fresh coffee rested in the air.
The writer and project now can begin,
Emerging words released by the pen.

Trees and roof tiles where wind can be heard,
An old ticking clock when we hear not a word.
A pool of light for thoughts to surface,
And sufficient shadows to reveal the circus.

Boxes of envelopes with part written tales,
Coloured stickers with thoughts and unveils.
Shelves with jars of memories and keep-sakes,
Speaks of adventure, trials, and heartbreaks.

Rhyming exercises that began just for pleasure,
Weaves into the line with added measure.
Background facts and storyboard layouts,
Perhaps a best seller, or thereabouts.

Times of dreaming between sleep and waking,
Finds a path through stillness and earth-shaking.
Our complex hero, more than a surface figure,
Closing the book, he may seem familiar.

Sleep Dreams

The Corridor – The day had been as uneventful as the weather, grey with little wind. I felt uninterested in anything. As I flicked through the TV channels, it seemed that the world had lost its cheeriness. I decided that the easy option was to head up to bed, turning the lights out behind me – surely tomorrow would be a better day? The bedroom was a tip. I had not realised, but this had been going on for a while now. A musty room with sweaty clothes left on the floor. It was not like me, but I had no energy nor the will to pull myself out of it. I climbed into bed the same way I had climbed out that morning.

Sleep did not come quickly, though thankfully, I was not troubled by menacing thoughts – everything seemed the same and boring. Sleep fell at a time I did not notice, like a thief that stole any possibility of consciousness or choice to move mind or body. The dream-maker approached and carried me down a long road with billboards on either side, advertising everything under the sun: holidays, cars, new homes, entertainment, and investments.

Suddenly, I was inside an exceptionally long and wide corridor. At the end of this corridor, there was a small window, which was the source of all light for those who lived there. There was a sense that the light from this window must never be obstructed. I could see many other windows along the walls, but these were mirrors reflecting only the corridor and all within it. Everything necessary to support life existed in the corridor, and for those who were there, things didn't seem so bad.

From time to time, the occupants would catch a glimpse of something beyond that small window. They were tempted to draw closer, creating an uneasiness. Quickly, they would return to the familiar mirrors, which reflected themselves and the existence of the corridor – a secure reference point in which they seemed to find peace and belonging.

I puzzled over the difference between the mirrors and the window. Should anyone pass through the window, they would find themselves somewhere completely different. This seemed a scary option. If dwellers were to try and pass through any of the mirrors, they would be right back where they started. The window is exceedingly small in contrast to what seem to be man-made mirrors, so large that they reflect everything – confirming their reality. They do not imagine it possible to pass through the small window. Though there might be just enough room for one person, providing they removed everything they had.

The window reveals light through a thin film

of glass. It cannot reveal things such as temperature, wind, odour, or sounds. People here can't measure how they feel about the space beyond the glass. They have no idea if survival is possible on the other side of the window. Could they ever believe their eyes?

There was a story here in the corridor that was rarely told about a boy growing up. He had a dream about a kingdom, just the other side of the window and insisted it was possible to go there. Fanciful stories were dismissed, and the young boy was encouraged to work, creating fine furniture for the corridor people. His stories began to create a stir as he became a young man – maintaining that the fullness of life existed beyond the window. The stories continued until one unusually dreary day. As the light changed, the corridor people decided they would hear no more of the young man's stories. They stripped him and threw him headfirst through the window – breaking the glass and the frame. And that was the end of that. Or was it?

Various people, particularly those who had bought his furniture, began to speak of seeing him again, walking and talking to others. Some said he had spoken to them.

Meanwhile, there was no glass in the window. Those who made the rules tried to have the window boarded up, but there was no other source of light, so inventors were called to create artificial light with little success. Rulers were quick to speak about wild beasts beyond the window who would devour anyone peering out. People had left broken remnants of his furniture by the window, like a shrine. The rulers felt this did not present a sufficient threat and chose to ignore it.

Often, you would see one or two people standing to the left or the right of the window, breathing in the air from outside the corridor. They seemed to come away contented and energised, though still fearful to speak of the other kingdom in public. Though in one or two safe places, discussions were growing about how, perhaps first, there must be an escape – but then a secret return.

I woke and sat bolt upright, ran to the landing window to see lights in the distance – car lights travelling along the main road and barely a star left in the early morning sky, save Venus, the bright morning star and bringer of peace. This was my hope. A new day and a new future to be part of. To step away from the confines of the corridor and to venture beyond.

Not Lost

Memories of the 3rd South Bank St Peter's Scouts – Mid-winter, and I had not been out for three days. Snow was lingering, and there was a bitter wind blowing from the north to northeast. It was the street-ice that was holding me captive. I'm unsteady on my legs at the best of times, although I had no real need to go out at all. My neighbour, Mrs Lawson, often pops in to ask if I need anything.

    I turned eighty last month and have been on my own now for almost ten years. Why do we count in powers of ten – the years go by quickly enough as it is, though I have learned to count and value each moment. A life span is not a straight line but many transitions that create our journey. If we are wise, we look to these moments as we would the contours of a map.

    Not that the house was cold, but the window view, white and crisp, made me shiver. I had a mind to rummage in the wardrobe for my old cardigan. As I said, I was not cold. It was just the feeling of being wrapped in something warm. This search had become a major operation. When did I have it last? The south-facing bedroom needed the light on as dark clouds drew in. The wall cupboard threw no light on such a garment, so I turned my attention to the large chest of drawers. The bottom drawer was so full that I could hardly open it. However, once drawn, it revealed so much. There was the cardigan. It's always a relief when we find the thing we see so clearly in our mind's eye – and to us, nothing else will do till we find it! The hours and hours I have spent looking for things.

Removing the cardigan uncovered a treasure. A plain grey blanket edged-stitched with green wool and tassels – as fresh as the fields. I pulled hard, for it was held at the bottom of the drawer, and I didn't want to empty the whole lot. My heart raced, not through straining, but excitement. Of course, I knew it was there all the time, but like many other things, I had forgotten about it. The one physical thing that has remained since I was a young lad – my Boy Scout campfire blanket. Now, that was much better than a cardigan. Drawers and cupboards were back in order, and I trod carefully downstairs to put the kettle on and make a sandwich.

The simple search took much longer than expected, but most things these days do. I sat in the armchair with the blanket around me, and while finishing my lunch, I turned on the radio for a little company. I find television demands more of my attention, and Friday afternoon is story time on Radio 4. It's like having someone else in the room, and I can choose to take notice or not.

JOHN PEARSON

I found little interest in the day's story as I took the blanket from around me and placed it on my knee. Here before me were so many stories from my years in scouting as a young boy and a scout leader. The blanket displayed various badges, of rank, achievements, and places. Those earned, bought, found, or swapped. There was considerable pride in creating a campfire blanket, each one unique. I was surprised to see how well the stitching had held – much had been done by my mother's hand and some by my own.

It was as if the radio level and even the wind outside had been turned down low. County badges of my own North Yorkshire and those swapped with other scouts – East Glamorgan and Berkshire. Proficiency badges – axemanship, sport, and reading. Badges of rank – sixer stripes and patrol leader. A sense of belonging – troop name and patrol colours. This is my material scrapbook, a map tracking part of my life's journey. It is a magical treasure in that it has the power to bring sunlight and stillness into the room. There is the sound of laughter and the crackling of a log fire. A fragrance of pine mixed with an earthy odour and that chilly air of the early morning when climbing out of our sleeping bags and lighting the fire for breakfast.

The use of knots has always been one of my strengths. Knowing the right one to use for the right task. Keeping the tension on a square lashing was essential, and knowing how the rope should best be laid enabled us to build strong bridges. All these skills were important, but it was working together that made the difference – knowing each other's skills and playing to them.

Leadership is knowing more about the skills of others and where the game should be played.

If I were to pass this blanket on to someone else, it would have to go with all the stories and emotions I remember. I should write them down, perhaps. Now, where did I put my pen?

Creative Thoughts

I was only seven years of age and staying at Granny's Farm for the weekend. Dad was busy wiring electrical sockets into one of the outbuildings. The farmhouse was in two parts: the big house, with Granny, Uncle Ralf and Aunt Margaret, and a door and passage linked to the lower end where Uncle Ed and Aunty Florie lived.

It had been a wonderful day down the fields and through the woods, imagining things that went on when no one was there. Then the long walk back for tea, playing Granny's old wind-up record player and sliding up and down the polished wood floor in the hall. The last job of the day was to fasten in the hens, only a short walk down the first cow pasture.

The light was fading as Uncle Ralf and I went up the stairs to the little room where I often stayed. I looked through the window to see the windmill before jumping into bed.

"Uncle Ralf, tell me a story, a magic story before I go to sleep." I knew Uncle Ralf had lots of stories, and he loved to tell them, too. These were not from a book but straight out of his head.

"Now, into bed, young man, let's think of a story."

Once upon a time, there was a young boy called William. His father was a joiner and made furniture, windows, doors and all kinds of useful things. William would watch his father for hours, working at his lathe, turning wood into something special.

He took a lump of wood and slowly moved it side to side with a chisel as it spun. First, around the outside, then shaping the inside, a beautiful bowl appeared. It all looked so simple, and his father looked completely at ease.

The game William played was to try and guess what would come out of the wood. On this particular day, his father was making four spindles for a stool.

William was sitting at a safe distance on a pile of logs, and it seemed as if everything was becoming further and further away. William felt a little dizzy, and as he shook his head, he found himself in a very different place.

William was still sitting on a pile of logs, but outside a cabin, in a wood he had never seen before. It was night, and distant stars were shining through a sky filled with colours of green, blue and purple. William could hardly believe his eyes. At that very moment, a voice said, "Hello, where did you come from?"

William held his breath. There in front of him was a small boy – though he seemed a lot older and dressed in greenery. William gasped and said, "I'm William, and I don't know." It was then William's turn to ask the questions.

He discovered the boy's name was Twig. He lived in the woods, though he was more a part of the wood than anything else. People would come from miles around, for Twig made some of the most beautiful bowls, plates and spindles. William noticed there was no sign of a lathe or chisels. He asked how this was possible.

"I just think about it," Twig said. "If you can think it, you can create it." Twig went on to give a demonstration. He placed a piece of wood on his hand and looked at it. The wood spun round, and a magnificent plate appeared.

"Here, you try," Twig said, and soon William was creating amazing spindles.

William felt a hand on his shoulder and heard a voice saying, "Come on, lad, wake up. You fell asleep." It was his father.

"No," William said. "I have been somewhere else, creating spindles by just thinking." William thought this was more than just a dream and wanted to know more about Twig.

My eyes were giving in to tiredness as it seemed Uncle Ralf was coming to the end of his story. "Will you tell me more about Twig another day?" I asked.

Uncle Ralf laughed. "Of course. I am sure that Twig has much more to say."

"Uncle Ralf, can we really create things by thinking?"

He thought for a while, and just as my eyes closed, he said, "Yes, I am sure we can. Everything begins with a thought."

Granny's Soundbox

Music has the power to enable dreams and much more besides. A change in tempo can move an audience from being gently subdued to sitting on the edge of their seats. The year was nineteen sixty-two, and the day of the telegram. I was eleven years old, and Granny's soundbox sucked me in and hurled me into a terrifying chase.

My family and I lived with Grandad in a house on Warwick Street, Middlesbrough. Garnett's lemonade factory stood on the corner of Warwick and Ayresome Street. The factory had not long been demolished, and as kids, we would play among the rubble. Ayresome Park was just over the road, and on a match day, you would hear us shout – Mind your car for a penny, mister.

The house was quite large, with three bedrooms and two extra rooms in the loft. There was no bathroom in those days, just an old tin bath, which came out on a Saturday night in front of the fire. The toilet, being accessed via the backyard – that's just the way things were back then. Grandad could be deemed a fussy person, a bit of a perfectionist, especially when it came to his joinery. An aroma of sweet-smelling wood up in the first loft room, where Grandad, following his retirement, would make small items of furniture. Granny and Grandad brought up eight children here, and the house had seen many happy days.

However, things were about to change as there came a loud knock at the door, a telegram for Mum. Dad said this could only be bad news. I heard mention of Aunty Doris, my mum's sister. I can just remember her, Uncle Bertie, and their little daughter Teresa, setting off for Australia back in fifty-nine, when I would be eight years old. We all went to Middlesbrough Railway Station to see them off. A large steam train rolled into the station, hissing, tooting, and a smell of soot. People were pushing and shoving, trying to get their luggage on board. The noise seemed too much as I pressed myself into my mum's coat. Increasingly loud cheering and waving, and the train started to move with long, deep puffs and a screech of iron wheels spinning on the track. Then they were gone, and all was quiet. Nobody spoke a word as we walked home together.

Dad was right about the telegram. It was not good news at all. Mum's sister had died suddenly. A great sadness descended on the house, as there could be no way that any of the family could get to Australia for the funeral or to support Uncle Bertie. Our house became very busy that day. Other relations came visiting, and Grandad just sat in the chair, his eyes all but closed, clasping an old handkerchief. Mum had me run up to the corner shop for more tea and biscuits. After a while, Dad suggested I go and play in the backyard, but I chose to go up into the loft room instead. My legs seemed to drag on the stairs. I did not understand grief. I just knew people who were normally full of fun, were, today, incredibly sad.

I turned right at the first landing, towards the second flight, my fingers touching the walls as I went. From the second loft room, I stood in the small dormer window, looking down to the street below, seeing more people I recognised heading towards our house. I turned around and sat on a pile of comfy blankets and cushions next to Grandma's soundbox, an HMV that had seen lots of use.

Lifting the gramophone lid, I found a record already in place – The Thieving Magpie. Tension could be felt and heard as I began to wind up the spring with my dad's words ringing in my ears, don't crank it too far, or the spring will break. How would I find out, and how far is too far? Seven full turns of the handle had proved sufficient and safe in the past, and it's best to stick with what you know. The music began with a long roll of snare drums, then the melody, and I became lost.

I felt as if I were falling and trying to hold onto something, anything. The music grew much louder and clearer, and the old blankets became lush velvet seating. I appeared to be in a VIP box in a concert hall with golden wood panelling. The orchestra below played the same overture, and the conductor vigorously waved his baton. Strangely, I could see no audience. Perhaps this was just a practice session? I knew I should not be there, and I had no time to try and understand why this was happening. I had to find my way out. Opening the door, I ran down an empty staircase, avoiding the foyer, afraid of being seen. I then found myself backstage. That's when it all began to happen. The noise of running came from behind, and someone shouted for me to stop. "He's stealing the music. Stop him," they cried. But as I glanced over my shoulder, I could see these were not people but musical notes – breves, crotchets, and quavers.

I grabbed hold of what looked like a blanket, labelled a Magician's vanishing sheet. I threw it over myself in desperation, and as the sheet continued over my head, I could see I had arrived somewhere quite different – a woodland stillness, except for a deep chirping sound, followed by a lot of chattering. My eyes followed the sound towards a magpie, a real loudmouth, feasting on a cache of bright red berries. I surprised myself to know his name, and was even more amazed to discover I could understand his every word. "You shouldn't be here," he cried. "They will find you. You had best follow me."

There was no time to share pleasantries, as I could hear the notes coming from my left. The magpie flew off to my right, and I raced after him – he must surely know the way out. There are times, it seems, when we must just trust. As if running with wings, my feet left the ground. Stranger still, I didn't feel out of breath. I still had speed to spare. The notes had also left the ground and seemed to be closing the distance between us. Their loud and tenacious shouting came from behind, and I feared them laying hands on me. There followed a long, hard chase as the woodland seemed to go on forever.

The magpie pulled up sharply, and I nearly crashed into him. "You must go alone now. Behind the waterfall, there's a cave. Follow the path and you will come out the other side of this mountain. The notes cannot follow you into the cave. Don't dawdle, for they will find a way around. Once out the other side, jump into the big river. It will take you where you need to be." This all sounded very scary, but I followed the magpie's instructions to the letter. A faint glow guided me through the cave, and I felt safe, not having the noisy notes behind me.

Once out the other side, terror struck me, as I could see many more notes than before. One grabbed hold of my arm, and I jumped out of my skin. There were two, three, four, five on me – each one holding hands with the other. A tug-of-war ensued.

"He is stealing the music. It's in his bones, don't let him go," they shouted. Somehow, I shifted to a major key, which confused the notes. The firm grip broke, and they fell behind.

As my speed increased, each one of my five parts collided, and I became one again. Realising I had gained my freedom, I began to run like the wind, jumped into the river and, like a whirlpool, began to spin. I burst through the gramophone door and arrived back in the room. It took a few minutes before everything stopped spinning, including the record. I felt quite dizzy, with a whooshing noise in my head. I tried to look around the room to see if I had been followed. My eyes were blurry, and it took a while for me to come to my senses. My thumb went into my mouth, and I fell asleep.

There are many twists and turns in family life. Unexpected cards dealt, and little experience as to how they should be played – adult issues and emotions and how a small child might interpret them. Often our stories become full circles and a learning process as they are retold.

"Grandad, come and see this." The year was two thousand and seven as I listened to the small voice of my first grandchild, my namesake, Robert. We were heading to Albert Park when a shower of rain drove us into the Dorman Museum, a magical place of curiosity and learning.

"What have you found, young man?" I answered as I turned away from the display cabinet and the gramophone player, just like Granny's old soundbox.

I found young Robert in the Nelson room, looking at stuffed birds – there must have been more than a hundred. "Grandad, are these all models, or were they alive once?"

"Oh, very much alive once." I stole a glance at the magpie in the corner and its (still) iridescent plumage and thought I saw a knowing look in its eye.

The first time I saw a dragon

Robert Giles, a young boy of seven, lived with his parents in South Wales. They owned a small shop just off the high street where they also lived. The front of the shop sold newspapers and simple groceries, but the back room was something quite different. Here, you could find a wide range of used goods and a bookshelf that filled the whole of one wall. In the backyard, there was a workshop where Robert's father would clean, repair and test second-hand goods before offering them for sale.

Before Robert's school days, the back room was where he played, and both parents kept a safe eye on him while they served customers. As he grew up, Robert formed his adventures and stretched his imagination, especially when he discovered reading books. As he began to read, he would ask his father about the big words, who would do his best to pronounce them in his Welsh brogue voice. From the bookshelf, Robert had five favourite books, but only one that he kept coming back to. It was an impressive-looking book bound in brown leather that he had imagined was dragon skin. The book was entitled, "All About Dragons". Now, dragons are mythical and magical beasts, spoken only about in storybooks. They have been drawn and written about for hundreds of years, if not more.

The book would speak about how their skin was as strong as iron and, despite their size, they could fly with ease. Breath of fire, claws and teeth were a vital part of a dragon's weaponry. They are the stuff of legends, terrorising towns and chased by knights in armour who would dearly love to slay a dragon and return with a fierce dragon's tooth. Stories also exist of dragon eggs with magical powers, and who knows how long a dragon can live or how long it takes to hatch a dragon's egg? Robert's understanding of dragons was that they could not be scary creatures because they were so amazing! Of course, we all know dragons in this form don't exist, do they?

School for Robert felt quite boring after his time in the back room. However, somehow, the time flew by, and Robert managed to do quite well in his studies. There was little work to be found in their small town, so Robert stepped into the family business and began to take the lead, allowing his parents to slow down. Robert's father would say, "This will be all yours one day, my boy." Sadly, that was the case, for by the time Robert was fifty, he was on his own, and running the shop in the family tradition.

It was late afternoon, and the sound of another customer was announced by the tinkle of the doorbell. A young boy entered with a piece of paper, and Robert inquired if it was a list from his mum. The boy nodded, handed it over and asked if he could look around in the back room. Robert agreed and began to put together a bag of items from the list.

Meanwhile, the boy emerged clutching a book, declaring he had some pocket money and was it for sale. Robert's family had a saying, "Everything is for sale except the family." Robert nearly dropped a tin of beans when he saw the book in the boy's hands. The size of the book covered the boy's face, and across the front was typed "All About Dragons". This had been Robert's book for many years. Was this now a time to let go and let someone else enjoy it? After all, what more could Robert learn about dragons?

Putting the last item in the bag and leaning over the counter, Robert spoke to the boy, "Would you like me to tell you about the first time I saw a dragon?"

The boy's eyes widened, and his jaw dropped. He could see that the shopkeeper was extremely serious. Robert began to tell his story for the very first time.

"I remember it was the Easter holidays, and I would be around fourteen years old. I went for a walk down through the woods and on towards the valley. Walking further on, I reached the part where the river cut through. There were many rocks, causing wonderful sounds of the water crashing and swirling around. I had rested there for a while, and that's when I noticed in a clump of grass a perfectly formed dragon – only eight inches or so."

The boy interrupted Robert and informed

him that dragons are huge! Robert was keen to continue.

"After hundreds of years, it had become necessary for dragons to be much smaller so they could survive. They move very quickly so as not to draw attention to themselves. It's as if they live on the edge of our imagination."

Robert continued his story. The boy was mesmerised, with his elbows on the counter and chin in his hands. "The dragon looked ill, his leathery wings swept back and limp. I instinctively ran for some water, with no thoughts as to what I had just seen. With the water cupped in my hand, I bent over and carefully lifted his head. The dragon began to drink and opened his eyes. They fixed upon me, and I could scarcely breathe as his body changed from dark grey to green, then to a sparkle. He looked at me, and I knew he was saying thank you as I felt the words inside me. My heart raced faster as I took in the whole experience. I expected him to be gone in a flash, but he seemed content to stay with me. Again, I felt I heard his words, Our secret. And I have never told a soul till today."

The young boy stood up straight, looked at Robert, and said, "You really did see a dragon, didn't you?" He thought for a while and then realised that Robert had said this was the first time he had seen a dragon. There must be more! There is always more, especially with dragons, no matter how small or large. All are perfectly formed down to their teeth, claws, and fiery breath.

The boy wanted to know so much but also knew he had to return home with the shopping. He asked the shopkeeper how much he wanted for the book and that he had two shillings. Robert was happy to take the two shillings and promised to tell more stories another day. "Remember," Robert said, "a dragon will always recognise truth and kindness and will return the gift with wisdom, peace, and all good things."

Petit's Pawnshop (1901-1968)

South Bank, or Slaggy Island as the locals affectionately named it, was a town built on iron ore from the nearby hills. This story is dedicated to the people of South Bank. People of determination, grafters who would endure hardship with a smile. Neighbourly folk, looking out for one another without a fuss – it was just the way things were. The story is fiction, though there was indeed a pawnshop on Nelson Street. It is written through the pen of a narrator – Elizabeth, who nursed Molly in later years and became very fond of her. Molly had clear memories of her time at the pawnshop, both as a child and later as the proprietor. Elizabeth collated these stories just as she had been told them.

Molly had been the proprietor of the pawnshop for a respectable number of years and her father before her. Known to all around as Molly's – though the name above the shop window remained, Josef Petit. She was born in

Whitby in January 1901, and the family moved to South Bank that same year – Mr and Mrs Petit, Robert at three years old, Martha just two, and Molly, still a babe in arms. She was to live at the shop till retiring towards the end of 1968. The shop had been there for as long as most folk could remember under a different name. A three-story building on the corner of Nelson Street and Middle Oxford Street, just across from the Globe public house. There was always lots to see in the window. Some of the items looked as if they had been there since the day it first opened.

This prosperous small town of South Bank had seen rapid growth through the industries of iron and steel, shipbuilding, bricks, and tiles. Thriving businesses centred around Nelson Street – people would say you could buy anything on Nelson Street: quality butchers, grocers, bakeries, drapers, and tailors. A pawnbroker is no less of a profession and an essential part of the community. This was a family business, taking great care of the precious items left with them, a temporary custodianship while the client rearranged their finances. On other occasions, they may never see that person again or learn of their outcome. Theirs was a financial service on a professional basis and they did not get involved in the emotional side of the transaction – at least, they tried not to. Molly's father was quite insistent on that, although she did notice a few times that he offered more than the true value of the item.

A pawnshop plays a necessary part in any small town, enabling people to borrow money by handing over something of value. After an agreed time, the item may be redeemed on the production of the pawn ticket and the money loaned plus interest. Items that are not redeemed may be sold, and the window displays a range of rings, watches, and musical instruments. Alternatively, a customer can choose to sell an item to the pawnbroker instead.

From her early years, Molly's job was to clean the items ready for sale and present them in the gleaming glass and wood cabinets. The window display, which faced the main street and round the corner, was her mother's forte. Whilst cleaning, Molly would find herself talking to the items, imagining it would bring them to life. It may seem silly to us, but she knew each item had a story to be told. Cleaning things such as a broach or a necklace, Molly would imagine them being proudly worn by elegant ladies attending a grand ball with music and laughter. She would be so caught up in the grandeur that it was as if she were transported to another world. Taking these wonderful items in her gentle hands, she would whisper words to them, not like casting a spell on them or anything, she just hoped that better days would come for their new owners.

People would often gaze into the window, and the old bell above the door announced customer arrivals. You would be amazed at the amount of stock, from floor to ceiling – furniture, lampshades, books, pots and pans, a suit of armour and some stuffed animals. There was a mix of smells, too. Musty and dusty, with varnish and a hint of potpourri. Molly, like her father, had a genuine mix of kindness and hard bargaining. The pawnshop often functioned as a confessional, disclosing indiscretions and infidelities. This would never be a gossip shop, for the community were trusting the proprietors with their treasured possessions and much more. The shop invariably had no more than one in at a time, which created an ideal location for confidentiality.

A Ships Cook 1907 (Cargo Fleet Wharf) – Molly was not at school that day. She was recovering from a nasty cold and pottered around in the shop. A Russian cargo vessel with a small crew had sailed in last night on the high tide, collecting a consignment of iron. The ship's cook had come ashore to buy some food for the captain's table. He was a man of some size, poorly dressed and with worn shoes. A straggly beard covered his neck, and in the crook of his arm, he carried some items wrapped in material and tied with a fancy knot. The cook had some personal business to deal with, and seeing the three golden balls, he headed towards Petit's Pawnshop.

The doorbell rang, startling the man as he entered the shop. Molly was just six years old and stood next to her father, who smiled and greeted the seaman.

"My name is Sergei," he announced. "I am the ship's cook. I feed the crew and the captain. I have some items to sell, please." His words staggered as he focused on this foreign language.

The goods were unwrapped and laid on the counter as Molly watched in excitement. Sergei caught her eye and admired her wavey blonde hair and blue eyes of wonderment. "Come," he said. "I have something for you. A gift from Russia." Sergei put his hand in his pocket. "This is Matryoshka. She is more than one. This is a family. A mother, her children and a baby."

Studying the painted image of the mother, Molly tried to figure out where her children were. "Here, I will show you," he said, popping open the outer shell to reveal the eldest child, then repeatedly until he held the baby. Molly wanted to know where the father was.

"Perhaps he is at sea." Sergei laughed. "I am going home soon to marry Yelna, my sweetheart. One day, we will have a family, too. Till then, I work in the galley where it is very hot. The pans go flying when the ship rocks and rolls." Molly asked if he would miss the sea when they were married.

"When I have my Yelna every day, I will be happy and have stories to tell my children."

Molly's father watched in amazement and joy at seeing his daughter's face. "Now to business," he said. "You have many nice things here. I will offer you a fair price that I hope we can agree on." Molly, by this time, was busy putting the Russian dolls back into their places and looking carefully at their faces and dress. There were two girls, a boy, and a baby. Even at that age, Molly knew that she would never see Sergei again, but she and the doll were never to be parted.

A Feather in his cap 1908 – There was always a sense of magic for Molly, growing up in this extraordinary shop – was it the treasured items or the shop itself? Her father would tell stories of mystical creatures, imaginary worlds, and little people who lived under the floorboards. Molly's eyes widened as she began to see more of the world's possibilities.

A tall gentleman in a warm overcoat and a wide-brimmed hat was trying to enter the shop. Her father called to Molly to get the door. As the door opened and the man stepped inside, he brought with him a gust of wind. The draft caused a feather to drop from the stuffed Pewit on the top shelf above the door. Molly watched as the feather floated down and rested on the gentleman's hat – she dared not say a word. He bid her father a good day, and as he lifted his hat, the feather drifted to the floor in front of him. The man apologised for bringing the feather in, and her father assured him it was one of theirs. Father spoke and said, "It is a rather beautiful feather, and it seems it has chosen you." The man thanked him and held it up to the light. He agreed it had great beauty and then placed it carefully in his coat pocket. Producing a small box, he explained that he needed some temporary cash for his business and would the shop be prepared to loan him two hundred pounds against this sparkling diamond ring. The ring had belonged to his mother. There was no intention of selling it and he was not asking for its full value.

Molly peered over the counter as her father opened the box. Her mouth dropped wide open. This was truly a large diamond, and the sparkle to her was like fairies dancing. Father was happy to loan the money, and the paperwork was completed. The man insisted he would return in three months when his business profits would surely cover the redeeming value, and he watched from a distance as the ring was locked in the strong safe. This would be something Molly would not be allowed to touch or clean, and she didn't see it for another three months to the day.

The man entered the shop and declared he was William and had returned for his mother's diamond ring. He pulled out the necessary cash and ticket as Father went to the safe and collected the ring. Molly held her breath as her father opened the box. The ring radiated light in all directions, and William smiled. "It's remarkable," he said. "My business has increased twenty-fold. I do believe it was the feather, it never leaves my pocket. I am eternally grateful to you," he said and left with his precious diamond ring and, of course, the feather in his pocket.

A cold December 1913 – It's not often that we hear of people's adventures and the inexplicable happenings that surround them. Molly's family beliefs, being that all things are possible, were so strong that they carried them through thick and thin. The cash flow for this kind of business was unpredictable, but there was a sense that something would always appear at the right time. There was one year approaching Christmas, with little food and the family keeping warm in just one room for a week. For the children, this was a great adventure, though Molly could sense the worry on her parent's faces as they shared unspoken glances.

The bell above the door rang, and Molly rushed to see who it was – a young couple holding hands, so close and intent on each other. They wanted to buy Christmas gifts for themselves and a few members of their family. They expressed a wish to find something old and unusual, a centre point item for their new home. By this time, her father had arrived and began to show them around the shop, assuming at first it was an item of furniture they were looking for. The story emerged as suspected: a newlywed couple who had been given some money. They wanted to buy items of interest that would last. They also wanted to buy for some of their family and friends, sharing their good fortune.

Father picked up a carved wooden box and placed it in the hands of the young lady. The expression on her face was full of wonder as she turned it over and over. Father explained it was a story box. The detailed carvings told a story, beginning on the top of the box and reading left to right. The story of love and tragedy continued over on the back panel, then on the left side, the front, and concluding on the right-hand side. Father was clear this was a copy of a medieval story box. The young lady said it was perfect and they would take it. As she opened the box, Molly knew what was inside – an old envelope sealed with black sealing wax with the initials W T. The seal was unbroken and as custodians of the item, it was not their business to open it. A black seal was often used in times of mourning.

Meanwhile, the young man was attracted to an astronomical instrument made from brass. He was fascinated by the many lines and inscriptions. Father, in his curator's voice, explained this was an Astrolabe, a handheld model of the universe. It was an elaborate inclinometer capable of taking many astronomical measurements and determining the traveller's position, longitude and latitude. It could even tell the time. The young man was fascinated. Father added that the origin of the Astrolabe dated back to 150 BC – though, of course, this was a reproduction. "We will take it," said the young man as he looked at his wife.

"We will take both," she said.

The couple went on to choose a few other items of jewellery and ornaments. When it came time to settle up, Father went for a box and some packing material. Before the story box was packed, the young lady opened the box and took out the envelope. As she was now the owner, she felt it was appropriate for her to reveal the contents. Molly handed her a letter opener and waited in excitement. The envelope was a sealed, folded letter dated the year 1815. The subject was a sympathy letter to a woman who had lost her son, 10th Hussars (Cavalry), at the battle of Waterloo. Already aware of the news, perhaps this grief-torn woman could not bring herself to open the letter, eventually finding its way into the box.

These unexpected customers brought significant income to the shop, which enabled the family to have a wonderful New Year.

They also felt, in some way, they had shared in the New Year celebrations with that young couple. The children's upbringing and experiences shaped their way of life, of service to others, patience, and trust, balancing the lows and the highs.

As times were getting harder, there were many looking to create some extra cash for basic needs. Then there were always those who were looking through the shop window for something special to take their eye.

Shaken out of our beds 1941 – On the night of the sixth of May 1941, all were fast asleep in their beds when they were suddenly awoken by a loud, sickening thud. They knew immediately what it was, for it was not the first time stray bombs had hit South Bank. Around the same time the previous year, a string of bombs had crossed the town, beginning at Cargo Fleet offices and ending at the South Steel plant in Grangetown. The family gathered in the kitchen – their instinct was to sit tight, for industry was surely the target. Mother and Father clasped hands tightly and prayed. There were to be more bombs dropped that following night, bringing the terror of war to their doorstep. Some lives were lost and houses damaged, but typically, the community pulled together as always.

By 1946, the war had ended, and her parents had turned seventy. They chose to leave the shop in the hands of Molly. Robert served in the Royal Navy, returning home safely to his wife. Martha had also married and settled in Normanby. Father was concerned as Mother became ill and needed fresh air, so they left to live with Father's elder sister back in Whitby. The reasoning was that they could look after each other. Molly was forty, and there had been no sign of settling down with a family of her own.

The Athelsultan 1950 – It was the 6th of November 1950, a breezy day but dry. Molly was invited along for the launch of a new ship by her good friend Minnie, whose sister Catherine worked at the docks. The launch of the Athelsultan was all about the dignitaries and well-to-do arriving in their posh cars – they saw two Rolls Royce that day. There were gentlemen in striped suits, trilbies, and overcoats and ladies wearing foxes around their shoulders, beautiful fur coats and fancy hats. Many of them went up to the grandstand area, where Mrs Formby would perform the duty of breaking a bottle of champagne across the ship's bow.

The girls, on the other hand, were standing on the dockside, Minnie and Molly, shoulder to shoulder with arms linked. The crowd huddled together in excitement. Father and son workers, wives, and family – a contrast of flat caps, head scarves and modest Sunday best clothes. All were focused on the ship towering above them – how did it not fall over? These skilful men had built an ocean-going vessel that they were proud of, as seen by the beaming smiles all around them.

Few heard the crack of the bottle, but suddenly, the dockyard was filled with the sound of joyful cheering. Mighty bangs as great blocks of wood were knocked out, and slowly, she began to glide down the slipway. Down and down she went – the rumbling almost drowned the crowd's shouting. Hitting the river Tees and pushing the water back, they watched her heading towards Hartlepool. "I hope there is a rope or two to hold her," Minnie shouted.

The VIPs were already coming down the steps, smiling for the cameras and heading for the hall and cups of tea. Catherine and the team had spent the previous day preparing the room with fine tablecloths and would be there in her white apron, serving guests and sponsors.

Minnie said, "Come on, let's go to the

canteen back door and see if we can catch sight of Catherine."

The kitchen was a hive of activity, and they nearly walked away when Catherine called out, "Quick, come in. You must see this."

The girls peered into the hall through the kitchen door – a smoke-filled room of folk and their finery.

"So, this is how the other half live," Minnie remarked. "Well, I would rather be in the Zetland with my friends. Still, someone must own these companies that put food on our tables."

Unwelcome Customer 1956 – It was late afternoon in mid-November. The lights in the window emphasised the darkness outside, and Molly gave a little shiver. She was about to lock up when a figure drew close to the door. There were just a few moments before the door opened, and the shape of a man entered. I say shape because his long coat had an upturned collar, and he wore a wide-brimmed hat. So, there was truly little to see of the person himself.

Molly called to him as he headed across to her left, away from the main counter. She asked if he was just looking and to let her know if he needed anything. The man mumbled something, but Molly thought it best not to ask him to repeat it. She explained that she was about to close but asked again if there was something he was looking for. The man said not a word as he made his way to the corner of the window display.

By now, Molly was quite uneasy. She was on her own in the shop, and it was dark outside, cold, and windy. This would not worry her normally, but she sensed something different here. Molly slowly made a move towards the end of the counter and reached down below, her hand grasping hold of her father's African club stick. She felt sure that this man was about to steal something and make for the door.

Suddenly, the man seemed to stagger and had to steady himself against the wall. Molly thought he was about to faint. She dropped the stick and rushed over, pushing a small chair under him and asking if he was all right. Molly removed the hat to find a young girl hiding. "What are you playing at, girl?" she asked gently. The story unfolded how, following her mother's recent death, the family had sold Mum's jewellery to the shop. This daughter desperately wanted the necklace that was first her grandmother's, back. The family had told her not to make a fuss – it was only paste. This was clearly out of character for the young girl, and the adrenaline rush brought on a dizzy spell.

Molly coaxed the girl up to the counter and sat her on a comfy chair. She didn't want to give her name, though Molly had a good idea who she was. From the counter display shelf, Molly brought out a mixed box of costume jewellery and popped it on the young girl's lap. She suggested the girl have a look and see what she could find. In half a moment a small necklace emerged, and the girl filled up with tears.

Molly's eyes also began to fill up. She could see the joy on her face. Molly explained that these were only paste and worth far more to the young girl than to her. She should take them home and keep them safe. This was to be their secret. The girl left, and Molly locked up for the night.

PC Davies 251, 1958 – The local bobby was a friendly sort and a frequent visitor to the pawnshop. He would be on the lookout for stolen property, not that a thief would try to sell stolen goods there – they knew everything was written down. However, if someone was duped into buying the goods, then pawning them was a possibility. One day, PC Davies came into the shop and asked if there had been any recent silverware left. Molly said she would look, and while he was waiting, would he have a cup of tea? The answer was always the same. "No, thank you, but I'll have a glass of water." As usual, the water went down in one, followed by a gasp and a thank you. Davies had served in the First World War Royal Engineers and must have seen some terrible sights – still, his light-hearted approach to life was commendable and respected by the community. He stood out on the streets, a good six-foot-two, then the height of his helmet. Molly would ask about his family but avoid anything to do with police business.

Emerging from the back, Molly carried a small box of silver trinkets. She explained that they came in just last week under the name Matheson in the ledger and said he was in a room on Jackson Street, number fourteen.

"That's Mrs Wilson. She doesn't have room for lodgers. Sounds like a false name and address. Can you remember what he looked like? This could be quite serious. The owner of the house disturbed the thief and was assaulted – he's in hospital."

Molly was shocked and went on to describe what she remembered. Quite ordinary, really, not tall or short. Not smart or scruffy. She did notice a rip on the brim of his flat cap, just above his right eye – oh, and his eyes were blue.

PC Davies was pleased. This was a lead. "Would you recognise him again if you saw him? We might need you to pick him out of a lineup." Molly thought she would and asked if he needed to take the silver. "Yes, sorry. What did you give for them?" The cost to the shop was three pounds and fourteen shillings. With that, PC Davies left, and Molly continued with her day.

The conclusion of this story came just two weeks later. PC Davies spotted a man fitting Molly's vague description while off-duty. The man was drinking in the Zetland public house and a little worse for wear. He was apprehended and, when questioned, blurted out his part in the story. Another man was traced and arrested. The victim, Mr Nobel, made a full recovery and offered to redeem the pawn ticket value in thanks for Molly's part in the event.

An Enchanted Pocket Watch 1961 – This was a bit of a shocker, as Molly related the story of the pocket watch. She had noticed a man standing over the road from the shop. She said he seemed edgy, looking towards the shop as Molly tried not to stare. She continued dusting and rearranging items. Glancing up once more, she could see him crossing the road. The bell rang as the man entered the shop and that's when she remembered him. A man in his late thirties had been in the shop no more than two weeks ago and bought a rather nice pocket watch. He had been looking in the window, and it had caught his eye. He had said he had not come out that day with any intention of buying a pocket watch, but he was taken with it. Molly could see he was agitated, shaking a little, pale and sweating. She wondered if he had a fever. His voice trembled as he introduced himself as Joe and began to tell his story.

On the day of the sale, Joe, a sharp-dressed young man (not at all like today), had left the shop happy with his purchase. He explained how he had not realised that this was a stopwatch. However, that also pleased him initially until he tried to use it. Joe insisted that when he pressed the stop button all time stopped, everything froze, even birds in full flight. It was fascinating to watch, he said. But then, that's when Joe's voice dropped, and his face changed as if terrified. The moment the second-hand counter had reached one full revolution, he could see dark, sinister shapes in the distance, heading straight for him. Pressing the stop button once more returned everything to normal.

The young man's voice strengthened, and he straightened his back. He swore he had done nothing to the watch, that it was enchanted – he wanted his money back. Molly did not want to test this phenomenon. She could see he was in a state and must have experienced something quite scary. However, a pawnbroker is not in the business of giving money back. It goes against the whole principle of the profession, but something had to be done. During the whole conversation, the pocket watch had laid innocently on the counter upon a faded velvet card. There was a slight hesitation as Molly offered the man half the price he had paid for it.

There was a long, silent pause as if time had stood still once more. The feeling unnerved him, and he began to look around the shop, perhaps looking for dark shadows. The silence was broken by the chime of a grandfather clock. Joe's answer came sharply. It's a deal. It now belongs to you. Molly had been studying his face and noticed a twitch in his left eye. She asked if he was all right. He looked a little pale. Joe told her he was fine, it was just that the last couple of weeks had been incredibly stressful. With a sense of relief, he took the cash.

The bell above the door let out its singular sound, and Molly was left looking at the watch. What was she to do with this allegedly enchanted timepiece? Immediately, she took it out the back, wrapped it in an old cloth and brought a hammer down on it hard. Still held in the cloth, she went straight to the bin and dropped it in with the other rubbish. The shop had gained half the sale price, which would be the amount the shop would have given to its original owner – one who never returned to claim it back. Molly wondered if they had a similar experience – something that would never be known. Father would say, there are far stranger things in this world than we can ever imagine.

Meeting Mary 1962 – An old lady came into the shop one day looking for a jewellery box. Within a minute or two she had told Molly a lot about herself. Her name was Mary, a widow living on her own, and Molly sensed she was lonely. She found a nice walnut box with rose marquetry on the lid. It was then that Mary told her how she struggled to see detail and how she missed reading books. Molly offered her the use of some old spectacles from under the counter, an uninteresting pair and probably 1900s. It was amazing to see the old lady's face light up as she studied the fine marquetry. She was so excited about the improved sight that Molly gave her the glasses for free. She left the shop with the jewellery box in a bag and the reading glasses safely tucked into her handbag.

It must have been just over a month later that Molly saw Mary again. She called into the shop to tell her how pleased she was with the jewellery box, but much more about the glasses and how she could see the beautiful rings and necklaces her husband Jim had given her. She then looked at Molly and said in a quiet voice, "Those spectacles are magical." Mary went on to describe how when she sat down to read a book with her spectacles perched on her nose – the words on the pages began to move and collect in a different order. The paragraphs she then read were all about her years together with Jim, things she had forgotten about or remembered differently. She said it was as if Jim was telling her the stories as he recalled them. Tissues, she said, were often needed – but tears of boundless joy. She was insistent that these old glasses were enchanted in some way. Her new glasses from the opticians caused no word movement at all.

Mary was keen to tell her about the sequence of events, how she and Jim met and how it all came back as clear as day. Mary was not meant to be at the village dance that week, as she was committed to being with her aunt. The last-minute change of plan and bumping into her friend persuaded her to go. Mary had learned the basics of the waltz, quick-step and foxtrot from her parents and could get herself around the room without too many bumps.

A live band were playing, and the village hall was alive with excitement. Jim arrived with his brother from the neighbouring village. Mary and Jim's eyes met the moment he walked into the room. She insisted that part may not have been true. Jim described their first dance as heavenly, like being in another world completely. She was able to count the number of toe crushes as Jim said sorry each time. She didn't mind a bit, for the touch of his hand and how gently he guided her around the room was wonderful. The evening continued with music, dancing, and talking to each other. Jim insisted on walking her home, which was a short distance but took almost an hour! Stopping at the gate outside her house, they enjoyed their first caress – soft and gentle, held in a long embrace.

Mary's eyes filled up as she told Molly her story. She offered Mary a tissue as she could feel their love so deep and true. Again, Mary said, "These glasses are magical. They are of great value, and I must pay you for them." Molly told her that she knew little about magic but did know that magic cannot be bought. If there was a cost involved, then it was in the things we let go of for the magic to emerge. Also, the magic itself will choose who it will work with, not the other way around.

Molly surmised that this was a simple case of self-hypnosis, causing a dream state in which Mary could revisit times with her beloved Jim. She was so pleased for her and whispered, "We'll keep it our little secret then."

Something in the air 1960s – The sound of Rock and Roll came over the airwaves, though jukeboxes were also becoming popular. We had Bill Haley and his Comets rocking around the Clock in 1957 and our Rock singer Tommy Steel in the same year. In 1959, Cliff Richard had his first number-one with Living Doll. Elvis, of course, always seemed to be there. Then, 1962 saw the rise of The Beatles, and the world went crazy.

There was never a television at the pawnshop, but always a radio in her parents' day. Music from the big bands, some light jazz and, of course, music from the shows. Molly remembered going to Scarborough, to the open-air theatre to watch Desert Song in 1963, South Pacific in 1964 and The King and I in 1965. She told of them taking sandwiches, a flask of tea, a blanket, and a cushion to sit on. It was tradition to walk around Peasholm Park afterwards, enjoying the fairy lights, before taking the coach home.

Around 1963, what sounded like a very loud musical box played the sound of Greensleeves through the streets of South Bank. Children would hear Lanny's ice cream van approaching, and they would run behind. Molly reliably informed me that the ice cream was exceptionally good, too.

During the long, sizzling summer of love, 1967 San Francisco saw an emerging culture of youth who wanted to change the world for peace. Hippies or flower people, in colourful clothing and flowers in their hair – we saw them here too as people followed the music and wanted to express themselves. Many had objections about the war in Vietnam.

The sound of Rock and Roll music was everywhere – keeping track of the charts and buying 45rpm singles from the local record shop became a way of life. So, too, did Radio Luxembourg and transistor radios. People listened in to commercial radio, in contravention of British legislation around the Wireless Telegraphy Act, to listen to unauthorised radio stations – I guess this made it all that more exciting. In March 1965, a UK offshore pirate station, Radio Caroline, sent out their first broadcast. There was certainly something in the air. We also heard news from home and abroad and became more aware of world affairs, changing trends and a high amount of change going on in opinions about how things should be. Father would say, remember when something is missing, and things only work to a point. It's at that time we need the 'in-bit-weenies.' They are the ones that would know what should happen next. The world seemed caught up in excitement and not always considering the best future outcomes.

The Bicycle 1965 – The song, 'Daisy Daisy give me your answer do,' came into her mind as she saw a young boy outside with a tandem bicycle propped up by his side. His dad came into the shop and asked for her best price. "I don't want it back. It was my dad's, and he doesn't need it now.

The wife and I were going to use it, but what with the kids and all… Do you have room for it?"

Molly told him the best she could offer him was ten-bob. "Can you do twelve shillings? She's in good working order. My dad taught me how to look after it." Molly gave in, and the bicycle made for two was brought into the shop. She gave directions to the boy and stressed to be careful and mind the display glass. The pair left the shop, and quietness descended once more.

With a freshly made cup of tea in her hand, she had barely taken her first sip when the doorbell rang again.

A middle-aged man was admiring the tandem. "That's quite a machine. Is it for sale?" Molly was amazed. The bicycle was still warm from its previous owner. She nodded and told him how well looked after it had been and that it had many pleasurable miles left in her. There was little haggling till the tandem sold itself, and within five minutes, they were gone. That had to be the fastest bicycle in South Bank.

The rest of the day was not without drama. Mrs McCelvey from Cromwell Road came in to redeem her husband's pocket watch. "He feels naked without it," she said.

Molly went to retrieve the item and asked when the baby was due.

"Oh, not till next week, by my reckoning. We have two boys, so we are hoping for a girl, but whatever the good Lord gives us will be simply fine." Molly returned to find the lady sitting on the small chair and gripping the arm tightly, tense pain written across her face. "On second thoughts, I believe it's today. Can you ring my Billy at the dock's office?" Molly insisted on ringing for an ambulance first.

By the time the ambulance team arrived, there was the cutest little girl, all neatly wrapped in ex-Army sheets, snuggled in matching blankets. Billy arrived in time to adjust his pocket watch and leave with the ambulance. Despite the drama, as Molly would say – you just get on with it. This had truly been a special day for both Molly and the parents.

A Milk Jug 1966 – A lady came in one day with a small brown paper parcel, beneath which were many layers of tissue paper, eventually revealing an old milk jug. The lady explained that it was given to her by a friend, who told her it was an antique and quite valuable. She had kept it for several years but didn't have space for it anymore. "It is Royal Doulton," she added.

Molly examined it closely and gently remarked on how pretty it was. However, she didn't feel it was worth what the lady was expecting. Yes, it is Royal Doulton and from the set Under the Greenwood Tree. Words around the top read Robin Hood in Ambush. The base of the jug had the number D3751. Molly reached for her reference book and explained that it was 1914, not classed as an antique. However, the handle had been broken and glued back. Then, there was also a large chip on the rim. Her best price would be thirty shillings. Well, the lady's face dropped.

"I have been keeping that, thinking it was worth a good few pounds."

Molly continued that even in good condition,

the price that she could offer would not be a great deal more. The lady's best bet would be to take it to an auction house.

The lady was visibly shocked at Molly's answer. She promptly wrapped it up and put it back in her bag. "Well," she said. "After I have taken such good care of it, being assured of its value." She marched out of the shop.

Molly did feel sorry for her and could understand how we all build up expectations beyond what is realistic. The fact remained that even at thirty shillings, the jug would have stayed in the shop for many years.

A Box of Bits 1967 – A young man carrying a large box struggled to get through the door, and Molly gave a little sigh. She was hoping for an early finish. However, she moved to help hold the door for him. The young man paused. Molly smiled, remembering him in short trousers, Paul McNee. The loaded box was placed on the counter.

"Yes, I'm Paul. I lived on Costa Street till my grandad died, then to the Dutch houses on Normanby Road. I'm married and work down the yard as a ship riveter. We're expecting a baby, that's why we need some extra cash. We've been clearing the loft out – Liz and me. I don't want these back. Just cash, please."

Paul was sweating. He would have walked all the way, and the box was quite heavy. Molly began to take items out of the box and line them up on the counter.

"These were Grandad's things from the last house move," Paul said.

A pair of nice vases, a pewter tankard, and a toby jug. This was not junk and would be worth a reasonable sum. Molly had learned how to remove emotions from business, and as she picked up a couple of silver picture frames, her voice changed. She was happy to take the frames but not the pictures. Paul nodded and promptly began to remove the backs.

Molly was in a bit of a rush to get done and wanted to get on with an offer, knowing that the money would go towards a pram and some of the many other things needed. Paul took out a small envelope from the bottom of the box and held it close to his chest. "There's these too," he said heavily. Molly looked curiously. "My grandad's medals," he replied and gave them to her. Molly opened the envelope, took out three medals and placed them neatly on the counter. Molly told him that one was the 1914 Mons Star – his grandad must have joined up early on. Medals do have a value, the star in particular, but she didn't often buy medals.

Paul looked at her. "Every little helps – and they were just in this old envelope and left in a drawer. What can you do for me?"

Molly thought for a moment and then suggested that she would do him a decent price on everything except the medals. If he wanted to sell the medals, he would need to come back another day with his grandad's story. Molly pointed out his grandad's name and regiment number on the edge. It's important to know all he can about him and to talk to family who still remember. Paul left with cash in his pocket, medals in his hand, and a project brewing.

Just over three weeks later, Paul was back in the shop with a smile on his face. "Hi, Molly. I have Grandad's story, and I wanted to let you know. I'm keeping the medals and the story together. I mean, how else will our child get to know about his or her great-grandad and all he did for the country and us." Molly could see the pride on his face and how tall he stood. His voice, too, was clear and decisive, the makings of a good father. She wished him all the best and to pop in with the new arrival someday.

Mythical Beings 1968 – Molly was beyond the normal retirement age and the sole occupant of this establishment. Marriage never seemed to be the thing for her, though not for want of trying. Her brother and sister had married and moved away, they kept in touch and Molly loved to visit. But her thoughts were now around her twilight years and how they should be spent.

As she was dusting, she picked up a special book. It had been part of the shop as far back as Molly could remember. 'Mythical Beings' was an old book even then. She would often take it to her room, first to look at the pictures, then to read the descriptions. She was told to always put it back when she had finished – everything was for sale in their shop, apart from the family, her father would say. These were incredibly detailed drawings of mythical creatures. Were they real or imaginary? To a child, they were very real and possessed powers that held the universe in balance. The elements of Air, Water, Fire and Earth – Molly could recall their names in that same order: Sylphs, Undines, Salamander and

Gnomes. She flicked through the pages and found them all still there – Golem, Cyclops, Gorgon, Centaur, Mermaids and of course the Unicorn. Their origin and reason for being helped to make sense of the world in story form. Resting it back on the tabletop, she gave it three gentle taps with her right pointer finger – half expecting the characters to reply.

Just as Molly was closing that day, a young lady with her son came in to sell some of her jewellery. A final transaction when in need of cash. Empathy, of course, though no judgement, as we are all responsible for our own decisions. While counting out the money, the young boy called over to his mum, can I have this book? Mum said she thought it would be a lot of money, but the boy persisted. Molly spoke quietly and told her it was two shillings and sixpence. She had seen the excitement on the young boy's face, and today, while dusting, she felt she had already let it go. The mother was pleased with her transaction, and the young boy walked out proudly with his new book. Molly smiled as she knew the exciting things that were in store for him.

Transitions 1968 – There is a time for letting go and moving on. Items and memories can keep us going around in the same circles when life wants to take us further out. Memories are never lost, though how we remember them can often change. Possessions become less important, too, as we get older. Molly hated the thought of shutting up shop and having a closing-down sale. She would rather find a buyer for the whole shop and its stock – to sell as a going concern. The area had gone through its boom time and was now on a rapid decline. People were moving up to the new estate at Whale Hill and houses were coming down. There had been a decline in trade for several years, and with austerity looming again on the horizon, perhaps now is the time to sell up. Plans need to be made as to how this might work and then to see what emerges. The property itself must hold some value. Molly had to admit to herself that the future of the shop was not in her hands. Her energy must be focused on finding somewhere to settle with her memories and stories.

 Her siblings insisted that Molly should take the full amount from the sale of the shop and its goods as they were already settled. The process seemed to have already started, and her brother was in touch with an estate agent. Molly did not like it when things went too fast, though she was grateful for the help, and this way, she felt things would get done.

 Over the following months, the shop no longer issued pawn tickets, and a 'Sale On' poster was in the window. Her brother was an immense help, taking stock to the local auction house. They had been advised to do it this way to attract a wide range of buyers for the property. The poster in the window seemed to draw more people than ever into the shop, resulting in many sales. It was an enjoyable time for Molly, as people she had not seen for years came in to wish her well and often left with a purchase. As goods departed from the shop, it took on a different tone. Sounds of movement and voices bounced around the walls, returning from several directions at once. The moving process was well underway.

Several interested parties had come and looked around the shop, thankfully accompanied by the estate agent. Molly was happy to step back and let it all take its course. Eventually, a buyer was found. It was unclear as to what his intentions were for the property. Molly had set her eyes on a new home back in her parent's town of Whitby. A small, terraced cottage on Church Street overlooking the harbour from the Abbey side – there was no looking back now.

Her personal belongings were boxed and ready. The removal men would take care of all that. The shop was empty and bare, awaiting its transformation, save for shelves and glass cabinets, the cash register and a strong safe, which were all in the sale of the property. She had laid to one side, the set of keys passed down to her by her father. Sleep that night was not going to be easy, as many things were spinning around her head. Molly sat up in bed and decided to write a list of all the things that were done and ready to go. She thought this would settle her mind, and sleep would follow. It didn't take long, for both her and her brother had done a wonderful job. She sat there looking at the list with its confident ticks at the end of each line. Suddenly, a thought flashed in front of her – what about the Borrowers? A book she had read to her two nieces. Bedtime stories about little people that lived under the floorboards and behind the walls. Items that disappeared in the house were borrowed to make the little people comfortable. This may seem nonsense, but to those children staying at that big house, they were so real. Surely, things go missing all the time, never to be found.

    Molly didn't remember slipping slowly down between the sheets, but as she did, she began to count the Borrowers around the table eating their supper. She counted five and watched as the mother carried the smallest one off to bed. The father told stories to the other two about his adventures in the big house. Molly, by now, of course, was fast asleep and floating on dreams towards the morning.

Daniel Gerrick's VR Quest

Introduction – Our hero is an average person, for whom the thoughts of travelling any further than between work and home were far from his mind. The desire to remain where he was far outweighed any curiosity that might arise. However, things do change.

The brightness of the universe willed him on, but darkness was looming and pressing in. His training had been intense, but still, the powers that rose against him were huge. Turning back was no longer an option, and his demise seemed inevitable.

Game alert! This story uses some computer gaming lingo – hang in there, non-gamers. This story is for you, too.

Outward Steps – If I were to write the story of Daniel Gerrick's life so far, it could be summed up in one word – uneventful. Daniel was twenty-eight years old, single, and still living under his parent's roof. He trained as a joiner and was very proficient in making quality doors and windows. People would remark, what a nice young man who takes pride in his work.

Outside of joinery, there was little happening, apart from his games console and VR headset. Any social interactions were via the keyboard – his Gamertag was "Doorkeeper". Daniel's parents tried to encourage him, but he was too comfortable in his digital world of both real and unreal characters.

His room was small, with a window looking out beyond the estate to the distant hills. Pride of place was Daniel's top-of-the-range gaming console and VR headset. The room was not as you might imagine, for it was tidy and orderly, in the same way he would keep his tools – sharp and ready for use.

A journey can start even before we know it – without a plan or a route, not even a destination in sight. Daniel's passage had begun without conscious thought or intention. No clue was given to its motion or direction, but slowly, there was an inkling that some unspoken message was passed to Daniel – and he unknowingly agreed to it.

We all experience and understand reality in three dimensions. However, Daniel was about to travel into the unknown, taking nothing physical with him, only his mind, wit, and emotions.

Sitting comfortably in his room, Daniel was viewing the game launcher through his VR set. His eyes glazed for a moment as if looking clean through it, void of any thought or purpose. What was happening on the cloud? A fear of missing out swept over him. His mysterious journey had already begun, towards emptiness and no virtual reality he had ever experienced.

The gameplay we are drawn into takes us down an inward path to the centre of our universe, a place to encounter our true selves and undoubtedly much more.

There was a shiver of nervous excitement around Daniel. A cloud of orange light surrounded him as the digital universe drew him into a place where games, yet to be created, were waiting in anticipation of the new game warrior.

Digital Conversion – Daniel felt, for him, that time had stopped. Though not consciously aware, he was entering the digital realm and being transformed into a string of binary code. Only as the string was de-coded on the inside did Daniel return to himself. His heart sank in abandonment as he strained to make sense of his surroundings. It was like walking through a fog. A new kind of awareness grew in this place where a compass would be no use nor stout walking shoes. There was no sign of any team players, for this was to be a solitary adventure. Daniel desperately felt for his game controller, but he was now on the inside. Trying to adjust his headset, he could feel only a metal helmet with sharp edges. This was too real by half. His avatar was tall and heavy, and it commanded a strong presence within his field of view. The big question was, who was controlling him, or did he have control? He tried button mashing, which created some awesome combination moves. This was going to be great.

In contrast, Daniel could sense the physical world left behind him, full of demands, worries, and what-ifs. Yet, here in the cloud, there was a feeling of safety – of not knowing/ yet knowing. His steps slowed and became longer. There seemed to be a purpose beyond his reach, and his curiosity was pulling him on. Not knowing, pushing him further and deeper without bearings. He began to question his childhood beliefs, the memories, and the stories written so far. Joys and laughter, sadness, and fears. A realisation that he was only who he was through his experiences to date. Daniel was convinced that there must be more than this. Why are we here, and where do I go next – can I create my future?

To which the digital universe replied, "Oh yes – from the inside out!"

Daniel was suspended at the entry point, sensing this was an action role-play game, when suddenly, a host of algorithms hurled themselves at him – a mix of scenarios – challenging him to move forward or to quit. There is a natural fear of the unknown, and the threshold between the known and the unknown is a particularly difficult bridge to cross. Daniel was entering challenge mode, and he held fast to the things he knew to be true. A double jump seemed to be catastrophic as he felt he was falling into the abyss. Down, down he went, voices telling him he was not good enough to go any further and that this would be his last game. However, Daniel's inner voice contained a secure ring and was just enough to enable his crossing – he was in, and a new scene appeared.

Experience Points – Daniel couldn't see, but he felt darkness pressing in from both sides. A cold stench in the air turned his stomach as fear gripped the core of his being. Instinctively, he pushed out his hands in front of him in a defensive stance. Immediately, light emerged from his fingers and streamed in all directions. The darkness withdrew, and a soft glow surrounded him.

Daniel discovered this part of the journey to be a training ground, encountering fears and releasing hidden strengths. Emotional battles from the past reared up in front of him – as real as they were, though twice as large. Confidence grew with each one laid low, dragons and demons alike. Daniel's pulse was racing, sweat pouring, and as energy ebbed, a new foe appeared. Thoughts passed through his mind – how long would this take, and how many more battles?

In this arena, time does not exist, and the rules of the inner universe differ, so Daniel must use them to his advantage. Pure and natural strength was forming based on clarity and truth. There also seemed more than enough room for self-acceptance and kindness.

Many aggressors of numerous sizes and guises advanced against Daniel. Eventually, each one fell to his sword or through sheer exhaustion of battle. He was beginning to feel invincible, though there were scars to be seen where wounds had been inflicted on him. Daniel became aware of an invisible force, both behind and at his side – alerting him to incoming blows. These skills are not taught but learned by doing.

The battle was won, and now was a time of quiet preparation before travelling deeper still. The presence of darkness didn't trouble him, knowing, should it come too close, he had the power to dispel it. Daniel's integration with the game had grown his confidence tenfold.

The Foozle (The final Boss) – Daniel took time to view his surroundings, the hills and valleys, dark forests and streams. He saw a castle and small dwelling places – though not a living soul to be seen.

An older voice seemed to emerge, "Well done, young man."

The voice reminded him of his father, watching over him as he grew. But this was Daniel's voice, stronger and wiser than before. "There is much more to achieve, and you must summon all that you have."

Though this was a gentle voice, it brought a sense of fear and trembling. His feet trod further on towards the castle, and Daniel felt the worst was yet to come.

Each one of Daniel's senses, natural and digital, were being alerted to a vile entity. He was already battling with doubt and fear, as from the castle gates, a large, dark, indeterminable shape advanced towards him. Utter darkness consumed this digital warrior, and he felt pain from cuts to his body. Daniel swung wildly with his weapons, though made no contact. His light was being sucked in by the darkness and reflected nothing that he could strike at. He bade up all that he had and threw it at what he thought was the centre of his adversary. It was useless. He was failing and about to be killed. Daniel's older voice spoke to him, "Let go of your sword. It will find its way."

He had no other option left – he was defeated – this was the end. Daniel let go of his sword as a fatal blow pierced his heart, and fell.

New Life – Daniel opened his eyes to see daylight and colours, a peaceful aura with sweet sounds – both natural and digital. His fingers touched the gaping hole in his chest and pondered on how this could be.

"Your enemy is defeated. You had to let go of the sword so that it could find its target. This is now your territory and your castle – you are reborn, one-up."

And what a life there was to be had. Daniel found that he could fly, soar above the trees and land safely in the courtyard of his castle. There was so much to explore within the castle – room upon room of precious items, treasures and, above all, a sense of wisdom. The unknown had become clear, and he had control of all this domain. His instinct was to remain here forever. There was no need for anything else.

The fatherly voice boomed out, "You can't stay here, boy. You have work to do in the real world."

It was such a familiar sound and one that brought back an aversion to authority. His child's voice would try to work around this instruction. "Just five minutes. I need to see more."

Foolish words, as minutes and seconds do not exist in this world. "These are things you can come back to and, in a way, take with you too."

Daniel had no clear way of understanding this and just wanted to remain where he was, just as a spoilt child digs in their heels and begins to scream. "You can't tell me what to do," he shouted.

Of course, he didn't believe that, but it was his way of showing his strength.

The ever-present father figure seemed content to remain silent. Had Daniel won the day? On the other hand, all this is inside and should be reflected on the outside. All of Daniel's learning can only be effective on the outside. He took his father's hand and began to walk on towards the second interface between the known and the unknown.

Return – He constantly looked over his shoulder, recounting the steps, the adventure, and the transformation. Then, somehow, the digital conversion happened in reverse, and Daniel was back in the room. Arriving at the place he called home, Daniel felt he must remember these things – life would not be the same again. There were new ways to be, and a new person was emerging.

He felt that this would not be the last inward journey. The sequence of events may be the same, though the dragons and demons will be different. He surmised that the skills needed would be linked.

Daniel noticed that he made more choices every day based on emotions rather than intellect and that there were still many things he didn't understand, but in a way, he was comfortable with that.

The game was over or was it? Daniel's life seemed to return to how it was before the first message. A memory is stored for future recall, though life once more became a little boring. His inner voice told him to be alert, for adventures often happen when you least expect it. Even in this place we call home, there is darkness and dragons of a kind intent on obscuring the real you. Back at work, and after finishing a job, Daniel got into the habit of leaving his doors slightly open. Potential thresholds to cross – portals between the outer and the inner universe, and, of course, we never quite know what's going to happen next.

Ugthorpe Mill (A Family of Millers)

Rising from its substantial foundations, twenty-four feet or more, this strong tower hides the cogs, wheels and driveshafts, each part skilfully made and pieced together with precision. This is our mill, taking the natural wind from the hilltop that turns the sails, transferring the energy down through the mechanics to the millstone. Here, the grain from our fields is ground into flour. Such a large contraption, when you think of it, to grind so small a seed.

The miller turns the cap to catch the wind, and the sails are set with just enough sailcloth drawn. The remainder of the sail, an oak lattice frame, creates turbulence as the wind blows through. This acts as a brake, maintaining a steady speed of around eleven to fifteen revolutions per minute – a higher speed could burn the grain. However, if the wind speed rose and the miller didn't apply the brake in time, the braking system would not be able to cope, and friction would set it ablaze. You might have imagined a miller's life to be simple and leisurely.

It is more than likely that there was another mill before the current structure. Records tell us of earlier millers at Ugthorpe. There is mention of a miller here, one Matthew Cook. Matthew was born in Egton in 1703, son of George and Jane (nee Pearson). Matthew married Elizabeth Durant, and they had five children. Upon Matthew's death, and in his will dated 1777, leaving to his son George the following:

My dwelling house wherein I dwell with all the stabling out housing garth and lands which I have... and all that my corn windmill situate at Ugthorpe.

George had learned from his father that just as the ears of wheat hold the grain till harvest, so the miller tunes his ears to the sound of the mill. There is much more to the drone of a mill. The rhythm has a set of sounds unheard by the casual visitor. Each tooth and cog creates a clunking melody, and the way the wind blows through the cap reassures the miller that all is well. Whilst working, attentive to the sounds, he is listening for changes.

Then, a sickening thud, a full revolution and there it is again! One of the cogs on the wind shaft has suffered some damage. This could be serious. If left unattended it could bring the whole thing down, such are the forces upon these wheels. Work must stop and repairs made good. A skilled joiner is sent for and arrives in haste. He knows the stakes are high in getting the wheel turning again. The flour must reach the docks in time, and there is much to do while the wind is favourable.

One day, when there was hardly a breath of wind, George was clearing up. A farmer came by leading a donkey laden with seven bags of grain, each bag around a stone in weight. He unloaded the bags, set them down by the door, and tethered his donkey to the nearest sail. The farmer did not intend to stay, but he and George got caught up in a conversation about crops. The miller jumped to his feet as the cogs started to turn. "Ey 'up, I didn't expect wind today." At that same time, the donkey began to bray with all the noise he could muster. The pair ran outside to see the donkey straining against the sail. He had walked across to try and reach a skep of carrots, turning the mill in the process. The farmer apologised and unhitched his donkey. "I'd best be off," he said, and George gave the donkey a carrot.

Sitting on this exposed hillside, the wind is the necessary element, but who owns the wind? Each miller has a right to have no one obstruct the wind towards his mill in any way. He takes grain that is not his and turns it into something of great value. He is paid for his time, skill, and the upkeep of his mill. A miller's toll can be around a sixteenth of the finished product, and there is a fine balance between profit, quality of flour and the upkeep of a mill. A miller is a key person in the farming community, passing on his talent and the mill to the next generation.

Time moves on, and the industry changes. The old gives way to the new. Ugthorpe Mill grinds to a halt and falls into disrepair, and the owner decides not to spend any more money on it. Eventually, it was sold and converted into a dwelling place. I wonder what sounds can be imagined by those who stay in her now – the wind, the turning of the sails and George whistling while he works.

I remember as a small boy, each Friday teatime coming over the moor road. I would be the first to shout out, "I can see the Minwill," followed quickly by, "I can see Granny's house" (Newgrove Farm) sitting in the trees just down from the mill. My imagination has always been much greater than my pronunciation.

The Travel Chest

It was a windy afternoon, and following Sunday lunch, when everything was put away, my mum and dad would take an afternoon nap – forty winks, my dad would say. I went upstairs to find a comic to read, or that's what I thought. From the top landing, there are four doors. Well, actually, there are five, and the fifth takes you up the back stairs to the attic rooms. All houses have an attic of sorts, a place to store the stuff you don't use but don't want to throw away – and that was where I found myself, the wind whistling in the roof slates.

My great-grandad George's wooden travel chest was sitting under the skylight. An intricate piece of furniture with many drawers and compartments, made by his own hand. This would have travelled with him through Europe and across to Asia. Dad told me many stories about George's expeditions and encounters in far-off lands.

I persisted as the locks were stiff, but soon, the great lid was lifted. I loved to poke around in the chest to see what I could find. Some old medals, a compass, a pocket knife, spare buttons and a dice. I played Kim's game, closing the lid and trying to remember all I had just seen, then opening the drawers and lifting out each separate tray – a set of drawing pencils and an old notebook. I sat back with the notebook and read how Grandad George had planned his expeditions down to the finest detail.

An old envelope had been caught between two drawers, upon which had been written a simple message – 'Matthew, write on this paper your hopes and dreams. Draw your imaginings.' Matthew was my grandad George's son. I opened the envelope and took out a small piece of paper, still blank, not a mark on it. Perhaps it had always been lost. I took one of the pencils and began to write and draw my thoughts, hopes and imaginings on the paper. It was not long before I had filled the page, and it was then that I noticed the paper was unfolding as if by magic. Twice, as it became four times its original size, the creases vanished. Amazed, I continued for a while to write and draw.

This became my special piece of paper that I kept in its envelope. After some days and more writing, the page was full, and again, it unfolded twice (without creases) to become sixteen times its original size. Now, this gave me something I could explore. I kept this secret to myself as no one would believe this magical sheet of paper.

A weekend away at Grandad Matt's house, and we were busy with a jigsaw, just the two of us. I asked him if he remembered an envelope from his father that referred to hopes, dreams and imaginings. He said he couldn't, but his grandfather had brought many things back from his travels. I explained how the paper, when full, opened twice with no sign of creases, and this happened twice. I now had a very large sheet of paper but didn't think it would open again. I felt terrible because the envelope was addressed to Grandad Matt.

Grandad thought for a while and then went to his desk. He brought out a beautiful pen of polished wood with ornate carving. He said, "I think that big sheet of paper was meant for you, and if ever you get round to filling it, then this pen will enable you to go off the page. You will write upon people's lives with the things you have to say – that's how change is brought about." I asked if the pen was magic, and he laughed and said, "No. The magic is inside you, and it has already begun to unfold."

Years have gone by, and the pen and the paper with memories and future dreams are in the travel chest. Life is fulfilled as dreams and imaginings become a reality. Everything is in my hands. However, I still, from time to time, look into the chest, perhaps to see if there is something still hiding there.

The Clockmaker

This short account was inspired by stepping into a small clockmaker's workshop on Gallowgate, Rothesay, on the Isle of Bute, Scotland, in 2013. Perhaps the story will help us value time itself.

Hello and welcome to my workshop. My name is Michael, and I have been a clockmaker for almost forty years. The formal term is a horologist, which I think aptly suits the skills and temperament needed for this kind of work. People say that when things are going well, they are going like clockwork. A clock relies on each part of the mechanism being precisely aligned – wheel and cog. The clockmaker must work with absolute precision so that his instruments can stay in step with time. Gears and bearings are set to move with such ease, driving the hands that accurately mark the passing of time.

The sound of the ticking clock comes from the escapement mechanism, measurably releasing the tension of the spring, allowing a consistent movement of its hands across the face. The sound of a ticking clock seems most at home in a waiting room – where time seems to be at its slowest.

A clockmaker is someone who is involved in the art or study of time, and I often wonder just how much time goes into the making of a clock. The process is not hurried, and the job is only done when it's done. There is meticulous care and attention to detail, making a timepiece something that will last.

As an apprentice clockmaker, I spent seven years learning the skills. During this time, I would build a clock for myself, putting into practice all I had learned, beginning with the drawings and then setting to work on the parts, engraving my design. I remember once it was done, sitting back and admiring the work. Time itself, of course, is invisible and is only noticeable by events that surround us, punctuated along our timeline. Clocks themselves denote the passing of time and, at each moment, advising us of the present. Advancing a clock will not take us into the future, but our imagination certainly will.

At this particular moment, I was sitting in the shop with my pince-nez glasses on the end of my nose, documenting the week's work in my ledger. The quarter chiming clocks announced four-thirty precisely as the front door opened. My first customer all day – she rummaged in her bag and produced an old clock.

"How much will you give me for this?" she asked.

It would have been nice to have had a paying customer I thought. The clock was old, probably mid-1800s and had a name inscribed on the back plate: James Harrison. This was not the famous Turret clockmaker, but I guess it could have been one of his descendants. This looked very much like an apprentice piece, with many elaborate markings (try-outs), ornate but not coordinated. However, it was a beautiful clock with quality written right through it. On the downside, this was not a production clock. It was a mixture and a one-off. "It is only worth ten pounds," I said.

The lady looked disappointed. "Oh, I thought it might be worth fifty."

"The clock will need a complete service," I explained, "and even in good working order, it will only make twenty-five pounds."

She began to put the clock back in the bag, saying, "I guess it is not worth spending any time on then. I shall put it back on my mantlepiece. It keeps my letters in place, and I am used to seeing it there."

I thought for a while and rubbed my chin. "I tell you what, I will give you twenty pounds for it?" I decided in that second if she said yes, I would restore it and keep it in my shop (not for sale). Perhaps one day, someone will come along and recognise the workmanship and its true value.

Just a Thought

A Thoughtful Warning
A thought emerges, lingers, then grows.
Twitching your fingers and moving your toes.
Our purpose to create requires first a thought.
For without this function, we are nought!
Stretching our minds and inspiring our hands.
Discovering life, and peace in our lands.
Use it or lose it, there's your option.
You will not miss it, till we've all gone, son.
Sionnan McMahon

Introduction – No one knows what's going on in another one's head. So, welcome to my world, a place where ideas are formed, re-shaped and emerge – sometimes as words, though most are held in the darkness of my inner crevasses. Thoughts appear as stories, an interpretation that hopefully others can understand. At least, that's my idea – there should be a purpose, don't you think?

My story is not set in a particular year,

though it is written close to the end of 2023 – in full recognition of the stresses and strains of current life. However, you are invited to consider this as happening in your present day, for I expect that little will change. A young boy is struggling with his identity and purpose. Later in life, he will be regarded as a prophet, someone with the ability to throw light upon that which is hidden from the masses. Specifically, in this story, a view of the impending destruction (or rebirth) of Humankind.

The known and unknown – We may be quite oblivious to the fact that we and our whole galaxy are travelling at 1.3 million miles per hour. Our amazing little planet circles the Sun at a speed of 67,000 miles per hour and spins on its axis at 1,000 miles per hour – no wonder we get dizzy. If this is so, then where are we all going, and how will we know when we get there? The truth of the matter is that we never will – because the speed is constant. Perhaps we are going round in circles, like cogs in a gigantic clock marking time. It's so confusing and fit to give us a headache. Then, the astrophysicists tell us it's much different to what they first thought. Sure, it's easier to believe that the Sun rises in the east and travels across the sky before setting in the evening. You see, if there are things we don't understand, then we will soon create a story that works for us.

Most people would give up at this stage, but bear with me – ground rules are important. Now the future does not exist. It's not something we can experience – it will always be just that, something forever out of reach. Often thought about, yet still to arrive, the old and the wise encourage us not to worry about the future – "It will happen someday, but not today." Many live in the past, and we know things certainly aren't what they used to be. So, we try to live in the moment and choose to leave everything to providence – whoever that might be. However, there is a need to have things in place, or at least something in progress, and some kind of plan as to how things can be. There must be a sense of, "We can do this" – but how, and who?

Sionnan of Corofin – I was christened Sionnan, pronounced Shan-in, the only son of Liam and Ciara McMahon. At seven years old a small prophetic voice was emerging, words heard though not listened to. With Colman, our border terrier pup, we grew up in a small town in County Clare, Corofin, by the River Fergus. Even as a small boy, I would often point out things that were not right. Trivial things, such as items in the supermarket being moved, seemingly for no good reason, and commenting on other people's behaviour or dress. I guess I was very much like the boy in the folktale, 'The Emperor's New Clothes,' I would just come out with whatever I was thinking. Dad said it was simply the way I was made, perfectly unique. There was a strong motivation to be who I was without concern for a correction towards the way the world, or at least how Corofin would have me be. ADHD had been considered, even something on the autistic spectrum, though doctors had no interest and just prescribed lots of exercise, which we certainly accomplished.

Do you see what I see?
What do you see in me,
That is your perception.
Who is it that you see,
A careful self-projection.
Others I can love not,
What stories they spin.
Caught up in their plot,
Curious, and absorbing.
Practised and familiar modes,
Guard us from things unknown.
Too scary to be on these roads,
Paths that are not our own.
Stress, living the expected,
Here we are, again!
How is freedom perfected,
My design is not the same.
I am perfectly unique,
Discovering me, appointed.
Life's amazing adventure,
So often, simply avoided.
So, fall right in,
Then step right out.
Endings are new beginnings,
It's you who creates the future.

The Burren – During these early years, Dad would drive Colman and me up to the Burren. We would walk for hours with the dog running on ahead. The Burren is a bleak landscape of limestone pavements, with remnants of ancient ring forts and dolmen (Neolithic tombs), upright stones with a flat capstone – looking a lot like a giant's table. This could easily be a scene from a science fiction movie and sparked many ideas that flowed into stories, and the word clarity rested well with me.

Dad and I would speak very little, but when we did, it was about age-old history and legends. "Colman," Dad explained, "takes his name from St Colman Mac Duagh, son of a chieftain who was educated and lived as a recluse on Inishmore, part of the Aran isles. He then moved on to a cave here at the Burren. He was summoned to build a monastery, a place of learning at Kilmacduagh." The story excited me as pictures of ruined buildings and hidden treasure streamed through my mind's eye.

"Can we go there one day?"

"Yes, one day," came the reply.

I knew that could be quite some time. However, these were great distractions and fuelled a young boy's imagination. Though there was an uneasiness in my head that I was unable to reconcile – I felt a deep turmoil that things were not right and that life was heading for disaster. Perhaps there in the Burren, things would become clear, learning from folk such as St Colman, a fearless man, willing to speak out and lead.

Stories for boys – Returning from one such outing, Dad gave me an old book, Stories for Boys.

"I've had this book since I was a boy," he said, "I would read a story every night. It helped me sleep – you should try it."

The book was full of adventure and mystery – I wondered how that would help me sleep. However, that night, I began on page one. A story about a knight in armour and his quest to find the lost crown of an ancient king. Three-quarters of the way through, my eyes grew heavy, and I fell asleep with the book still open on the bed. The following night, I returned to the story, only to find that the knight was rescuing a young peasant girl who had fallen into the river. Heading to the beginning of the story, I found it was all so different. Turning the book over and over, I looked to see how this could have happened – it was just a normal book, yet last night's story was nowhere to be found. Again, I fell asleep before finishing the story, and again, the story had changed by the following night. This was infuriating and taxed my mind. "Dad, what's going on with this book?" I explained the best I could.

Dad frowned. "I don't know. I used to read a whole story every night – you need to finish what you started."

The next night, I climbed into bed and found a new story. I began to pinch myself at the end of each line, making sure I didn't fall asleep. The story was completed, and I had the best night's sleep ever.

At breakfast the following day, I announced, "I've been thinking."

Dad looked up. "That's good, son. It proves you exist as a person – I think; therefore, I am, (Descartes)."

"I must have dreams mixed up with reality. Stories in books can't just change. But it seemed so real."

"If there's a reason to doubt the truth, then it must be discarded as false. We soon realise that there is little that can be relied upon, particularly our dreams." Dad continued to eat his breakfast while Mum cleared the pots.

Dark Times – Ten years of schooling was summed up by the deputy head, Mr O'Brien: "Sionnan can go much further, even university. He would be, by far, the top of his class. However, he tends to overthink things, asking question after question. Why he cannot just accept what he is taught is beyond me. He distracts the other students and drives me up the wall. I recommend he goes to college and find a trade in engineering. That'll keep him occupied." Dad agreed, knowing what I was like at home, too.

Schooldays were left behind, and a short stint at college followed. Try as we may, no work or apprenticeships could be found. I spent much of my time in thought, wrestling with ideas. Attempts to join a local political group failed, as no one wanted to listen – my ideas were still unclear. How could I then explain them to others? A blog page and YouTube channel only attracted fringe weirdos. The impact intended fizzled, and I felt I needed a bigger stage. The things that I could see in the future were often too frightening to put into simple words.

The story that grew throughout my life revealed what I could see as the potential destruction of Humankind losing the ability to think. How we are consumed and rely upon the information network, we call the internet, which could implode, leaving nothing. This is not a conspiracy leaving a victor/ dictator/ ruler – it is the ultimate annihilation of everything.

For Humankind has an inbuilt need to

create. Thought is essential to creation, existence, and the continual development of our being. Our thoughts are stimulated by observations and events within reality, emerging from our imagination of how things can be – a drawing board, a place where we would refine our theories.

Information (data) is the new currency and a reliance on having everything at our fingertips. We are suffering from information overload, and most of it is senseless. Humankind is consumed by a total distraction from living. We are losing the ability to think, and everyone seems to follow blindly like sheep. This infuriated me. Why could they not see the better path?

I never saw myself as a prophet, but I held a model of a world built on numerous levels. The physical, emotional, practical, scientific, social, and spiritual. Technology has moved so fast that it still seems to be accelerating. There is an underlying belief that anything can and will be achieved, from interplanetary travel to irradicating diseases. Even the threat of global warming and natural disasters seems less of a worry to people today.

A message seemed clear in my head, though still difficult to put into words that others could understand. The future of Humankind was at stake. This was not an issue of economic collapse or global warming, though, in my vision, these concerns would also be dealt with. I still could not understand why I was being ignored, dismissed, and often ridiculed. People seemed more consumed with trivial issues – creating mountains and not seeing the futility of it all.

In my deepest belief, I felt that nature would recover because of its inbuilt network of 'survival impulses.' As we become aware of our survival impulses, then the original plan for us will be fulfilled. However, some seem hell-bent on keeping this portal closed, seeing it as a threat to their position. Although this line of thinking has all the hallmarks of a conspiracy theory, folk will not give it time for serious thought.

Space to think – I progressed from a bicycle to an old motorbike, continuing to visit the Burren with Colman strapped to my back in a holdall. The wind across the Burren holds a particular sound as it blows through the empty land – a space just to exist, expectantly waiting for thoughts to arise. There are signs of life in this barren wasteland. Rare plants thrive here and nowhere else. Sitting in emptiness, words and pictures invaded my mind – of demons coming to steal away my thoughts. I found it easier to speak out loud. No one was there to disagree with me, apart from myself. I was reaching desperation.

"Why do people look strangely at me, look at each other and then laugh? I wish I could disappear into another world where there is kindness and acceptance. Why is it only me who feels this way?" Nothing but silence, no answers, simply more questions.

Dark clouds were moving in from the sea, and that wind was cutting right through me. I was unable to move. Some unknown force held me fast as volumes of emotion rose from within. "What about me?" I shouted with all the breath that I possessed. "Where do I fit in? Do I even matter?" Colman's head tipped to one side, and his ears lifted attentively, which calmed me slightly. The outburst was essential, letting off pent-up steam, and my inner voice uttered many expletives, too.

Back home in the garden shed, I engrossed myself in art as a medium to express my prophetic mission. These images were so dark and imposing that people turned away. In a fit of rage, I set fire to all my pictures and sunk into depression. My parents were not equipped to support me in this matter, and things were looking bleak. Dr Finn tried to reason with me, but in my opinion, the doctor's knowledge all came from books, without a true understanding of people. It was Uncle Darrah who spent time with me, giving me the space to be just me – often there in the garden shed, among the disorganised mess of writing and sketches, models, and complex structures – to outwork my visions.

Fear
There are things I am afraid of,
Others stir a laugh.
Expecting then mistaking,
Declared only by half.
In the corners of my being,
I know that things are wrong.
Transpires from my unseeing,
Now where does that belong?
In the depths of my fears,
There seems no escape.
No valleys or still waters,
Then am I truly awake.
Living life inside out,

All about existence.
Finally at the check-out,
No place for resistance.
Will it all become clear,
A turning point in creation.
Announcing a new frontier,
To one, eternal nation.

Daybreak – A stirring emerged within me as, resting in and among the internet clutter, I discovered a quotation.

"Out beyond the ideas of wrong-doing and right-doing, there is a field. I'll meet you there."

A quotation ascribed to Rumi.

I interpreted this as a call to the old monastery at Kilmacduagh, a place I had yet to visit. Dad had told the story of Saint Colman, walking through the woods of the Burren when his girdle fell to the ground. Taking this as a sign, he built his monastery on that spot. The girdle was said to be studded with precious gems. So, I set off with Colman that same day. The first sight of the monastery, known as the seven churches, quite took my breath away. Motionless, I surveyed the ancient site, feeling this was a significant place, a doorway to my future. Colman was off, darting from one side to the other as new smells drew him further on.

Then, standing tall and proud among the gravestones, I gazed at the round tower – reaching almost a hundred feet and presenting a distinct lean. Strangely, the only access door stood some twenty feet above ground level – how on earth would anyone get up there? My feet were drawn towards the round tower but turned partway as the doorway to the cathedral drew me inside. Empty and bare, the walls no longer supported a roof, and I sat in wonderment at the peace that surrounded me. A true calm descended – not something I had felt before – disturbing thoughts were nowhere to be heard.

I struggled to get my head around how beautiful it was here and that there were no visitors today. Surely, folk would come from miles around to help restore their peace and recharge their emotional batteries. But no, people are too busy arguing and holding on to things that are not necessary – when will they learn? Within this peaceful environment, a new thought began to grow. When I slow down, things look better. What if I could slow down sufficiently – that I could watch the stars float across the sky or plants growing? Stars look remarkably still, as if frozen in time. I know they are moving, but my eyes deceive me, the same with plants and trees.

The Stone – Colman was laid with his neck stretched across the top of my right leg – an ear twitching, listening to every word. He knew that if his master moved, he would know about it and wake immediately. I rummaged in my pocket, for when we first arrived, and Colman was set on the ground, I had picked up a stone, rubbed it between finger and thumb, and popped it in my pocket – something I would often do. Bringing the stone out into the light of day and placing it in the palm of my hand, I noticed the stone seemed a soft sedimentary rock, crumbly to the touch, and as I rubbed it, flakes fell from it. The rubbing was not intentional, more as a distraction. However, with each push of my thumb, a groove was being worn into the rock – down to a point when the texture changed. This drew my attention to the stone, and I could see a deep blue colour inside this grubby rock.

Further scratching and fierce rubbing revealed a hidden gemstone, oval and about an inch and a half at its widest point and three-quarters of an inch thick – what a treasure. Remnants of the monastery were lost in mud for fifteen hundred years perhaps. The sound of flowing water led me down to the stream, where I washed the stone and polished it with my handkerchief. Holding it up to the sunlight and squinting through its deep blue colours, there seemed to be a mist swirling. I decided this was a truth stone, and there was no notion as to where this thought had come from, but it made sense. It was as if the stone was speaking, reassuring me that all was well. My self-confidence rose above the fears as a new light flooded my consciousness. Fresh words appeared, forming clarity and inspiration – I reached for my notebook and began to write words before they were lost, initially making no sense at all.

Poems from the Heart – This old notebook was kept for my eyes only, and at this point, I regarded them as wise words – perfect and born out of deep need. Some of these words had rhythm, and some even rhymed. I felt sure these were not my words but emerging through the stone from some far-off time when things were quite different, or were they? Part of the issue was around judgment, and I could feel the tension and challenge of these words:

Are we not fortunate to have, the freedom to make judgements?
From the confines we've created, of this, relatively comfortable life.
Creating a story, we often think fits, of what is happening around us.
Defying the truth and goodness, preferring our needs over others.
Humankind's default position, the eternal horror of man unto man.
To judge without knowledge or care, even under the banner of our God.
To realise at my deepest level, you are my brothers and sisters.
There can always be reconciliation, a space and time for peace.
I accept the responsibility, for my immediate universe.
Those around me, my family, and friends, for change, can only begin with me.

This was something new, bold yet palatable that all may digest. It will always depend on those who read or hear it – but if they hear it, they will. My truth stone was a treasure to be kept safe, and I told no one about it. In my imagination, it was magical, mystical, and probably from St Colman's girdle.

Kavanagh's Bar – Uncle Darrah heard about a job serving behind the bar at the local public house. I am sure he put a good word in for me, and soon I was pulling pints. Most would say this was a bar full of drunken old fools who would talk about anything and anybody, each one having their own opinion and not one wishing to change. Peace reigned by allowing everyone to linger where they were. I would be drawn into their conversations, and soon, I was learning to choose my words wisely. After only a few short weeks, as folk arrived in the early evening intent on washing down the dust of the day – I would be asked, "What's the question of the day, Sionnan?"

"Ah well," I would begin. "I was thinking just this morning…"

"You can be arrested for that now, Sionnan." The men would laugh – then listen intently for my next sentence, knowing I had their attention.

"I was thinking, how did we get as far as this without realising where we are going."

"Well, if I was going to Galway, I wouldn't catch a bus to Limerick, though the way my wife drives, I could end up anywhere." The weird and wonderful comments would roll off their tongues until they had exhausted all possibilities.

Then, a question from the group, "Where are we going?" A serious question that again followed humorous answers.

"Well, I'm not going home till I have had at least two more beers."

And another, "Will it be heaven or hell? We'd best ask the priest," followed by raucous laughter. When the humorous and weird replies were done, more philosophical conversations emerged, though not wishing to make a definitive statement.

After a while, I began to read some of my written words. I think they were well received – of course, I told myself that they were just being polite. The response from the locals, a round of applause, left me clueless as to what, if any, impact had been made. Coming to the bar one at a time, they would ask personal questions regarding some part of the poem.

Then, the one that I had named Micky Finn asked, "Tell me more about that last poem, Sionnan. It keeps ringing in my head."
My words from the Burren were sinking in and changing people's thinking.
Nature fits like a glove,
All are vital to each other.
No need to push or shove,
A full expression of mother.
Linguistic love and sacrifice,
Harmony in life and death.
Creates not the throw of a dice,
But sustains every breath.
War dressed up as protection,
Nothing but destruction,
Without any calculation,
And endless repetition.
Hatred shortens life,
Greed shifts the balance.
Man has surely lost it,
Not knowing all he had.
Forbidden fruit upheaval,
The tree of life and knowledge,
Of all that is good and evil,
Played out upon this stage.

Ending – When nature is left to its own devices, it seems to be able to recover from pretty much anything, given time. Take time then to learn from the universe, the things we often overlook. There are blind alleys and detours, and we are attracted by shiny objects and fancy treasures. Artificial intelligence – c'mon, the clue is in the first word.

Today is where the writer of this story leaves the book. A story, of course, is just a story – though it can also illustrate profound truths. The future is dependent on Humankind, which means you. How do our thoughts affect the rest of the world? Like ripples on a pond, they continue to the far edges of reality. Choose words wisely, for our actions must be congruent with our new thoughts.

Exercise your creative self and use your given gift to THINK. Process and put into action in all aspects of life. Create the story and live it. Refuse to be drawn into the dross of what people regard as the norm. Do not be afraid to speak out. Invest time in yourself, you will be amazed at what you will discover and who you will become.

The Ghost

Words fell upon the page as Andrew began to write:

Brenda had attended a séance and was walking home alone. The night air was cold and thin, as strange sounds came from the avenue – something was coming towards her. Fear was ahead and behind her. It seeped into her very being and removed all sense of reasoning. This intelligent woman became a gibbering mess, wanting to run yet unable to move her limbs. Disconnected, with no rationale for what was occurring, fear escalated to terror, bringing with it uncontrollable shaking. Her inner scream was stifled by contracting sinews in her neck as the spectre pointed a crooked finger towards her.

Andrew scrunched up the sheet of paper, threw it towards the bin and lit another cigarette. The small electric fire struggled to heat his bedsit, and an empty whisky bottle that he could not remember drinking lay on the floor.

Life as an independent journalist was hard.

Andrew was low on cash and needed a good article for local reading. He had been out drinking in Leeds the previous night and got into a conversation about ghosts – do they or don't they exist? A heated debate followed, with stories of apparitions and objects thrown. Those who were there could express accounts witnessed by people they knew.

For all his forty-nine years, Andrew was clear in his mind that ghosts fell into the same category as fairies and aliens. Having spent most of the night between sleeping and waking, he was finding it difficult to write about something he didn't believe in. However, he couldn't deny the strong opinions of people, even though the year was now 1964. These people would also be readers of the Leeds Mercury, his only source of income. All Andrew had to do was to make something up. No one could argue otherwise.

Without washing or shaving, he threw on his overcoat, scarf, and trilby and headed out towards the tobacconists. Once the new pack of twenty was safely in his pocket, Andrew decided to turn and head out into the country. He felt that a short walk of around three or four miles would do him good and clear his head. The route would take him up a hillside where he could sit and look out across the valley, a place he had often walked.

It was a cold November morning, though there was shelter from the hillside as he sat on a wooden bench and took in the view. Andrew decided to begin his article from a position of non-belief. He warmed his hands by rubbing them together, pulled out his pencil and notepad and began to write.

There has never been any conclusive evidence found that proves the existence of ghosts. It seems strange that all reported activity has been at night when our eyes can easily be deceived – do ghosts only come out at night? Why is the focus always on the witching hour of midnight? Do ghosts carry a timepiece? He laughed to himself.

There are so many things we believe without good reason. For example, we touch wood, fear breaking mirrors or cats walking across our path – we call this superstition. On the one hand, we laugh at superstition, yet we play along with it, not wanting to tempt fate.

But what is it that's behind you? Until you spin around and see nothing. Those times when the hairs on the back of your neck prickle and send cold shivers down your spine. Everything about you is on 'Red Alert,' adrenaline coursing through your body, preparing you to fight or flee.

Some people believe in aliens, fairies, and leprechauns, and some even believe that the world is flat. We are surrounded by lies painted in beautiful colours, each deception having an element of possibility, drawing us into a counterfeit world.

Andrew placed his pencil and notepad into his coat pocket as his gaze was drawn towards several small twigs that were being moved by the wind. He would have expected them to continue past him, but they seemed content to remain within his reach. A strange chill passed through every bone in his body, causing him to shiver violently. He imagined this was the aftereffect of the whisky and wrapped his arms around his chest, breathing deeply. Warmth returned, but the sounds of wind through the tree branches grew louder until he needed to clasp his ears with both hands. With eyes tightly closed, he spoke to himself in a quiet voice. "It's all right, Andrew, it's just the wind." The voice was reminiscent of his mother, reassuring her young child.

Opening his eyes, the twigs were motionless, and something inside him spoke the word, 'Hello.'

Something or someone was speaking to him in a way he could never have imagined. As if shuffling dominoes, Andrew wiped his hand over the twigs and spoke out loud. "Who are you?"

The twigs moved once more of their own accord. "My name is Oswald Thompson."

By now, the prickling hair on the back of his neck sent chilling signals throughout his body. His heart was pounding, and his senses were somewhere between fear and curiosity. Apart from the physiological shaking and tingles, he felt strangely calm. This was not a hangover experience but a ghostly encounter. Although not the kind of spiritual activity spoken of the night before. Andrew was compelled to ask the ultimate question. "Are you alive or dead?"

The group of twigs moved frantically, almost lifting off the ground before coming to rest. "Dead to your world, alive to this." This unholy conversation with a spiritual being continued.

"When did you die in this world?"

Andrew pieced together the following sentences and frantically wrote them on his pad.

"1873. An accident at Lower Edge Mill. The conditions were hard, and the mill owners were pushing for profit. I left a widow and five small children. God only knows what happened to them."

Andrew was distressed and lost for words. "I am sad to report that in ninety years, very little has changed in the way of man's greed."

At that moment, the wind dispersed the twigs, and all was lost. Andrew was certain he had not dreamt it, for he had his notes and now a story to write. There was a hunger in his belly that included breakfast as he set off for home.

It was midday before Andrew felt presentable to the world, and he caught a bus to the Mercury newspaper offices. The place was a hive of activity, everyone in a rush to meet print deadlines. He stayed away from the busy news section and avoided awkward conversations with people who would pester him for work with no pay. Andrew headed for the archive department and spoke softly to the admin girl.

"Hi, Susan, am I okay to spend an hour or so in here?"

"Sure, Andrew, help yourself," she said without even looking up.

Andrew lifted down a cold tin containing microfilm dated 1873, loaded it onto the machine and began to reel through the data.

He fumbled in his pocket for a cigarette and was politely reminded by Susan. "Sorry, no smoking in here."

His eyes blurred as the information scrolled down the screen until, eventually, he came to – Death at Lower Edge Mill, and he read:

November 1873. The first inquest was held into the death of Oswald Thompson, who was employed at Lower Edge Mill. Mary Shaw, a minder at the mill, was called, and she stated that on the Tuesday morning, the feed that Thompson had to keep flowing was stopped, and he went underneath the lapping machine, which was still in motion, to try and fix it. Her attention was then distracted elsewhere.

Alexander Hardgrave, carding master, was next called, and he stated that he had been called to the lapping machine, where he found the deceased below it. He observed that his head was beneath the machine, one part of which was stopped and the other part still revolving. His waistcoat was lapped hard around the second driving shaft. It had pulled his body up to the top of the shaft, and he was quite dead. His neck was black and swollen, and his hands were bruised. He had no business going under the machine while it was running.

Andrew's head was spinning as he transcribed the exact words to his pad. This proved his experience with Oswald and the twigs. It was all true. He felt he had stepped to the edge of the unknown and reached in. But how was he going to tell the story? He wanted to touch both the ghost hunters and the sceptics to tell them, once and for all, that ghosts exist.

However, he pondered the moral obligation of journalism, a responsibility to keep people safe in mind, body and spirit. The code of ethics dictates: speak the truth and report it, minimise harm, act independently, and be accountable. Andrew's accountability at present, was to his landlord and paying his previous month's rent. He also felt Oswald's pain leaving behind a young family – ripped from this world so cruelly, trying to keep a machine working to earn the money they needed.

Andrew had in his mind to seek out Oswald's descendants and grandchildren. That would be an enormous task, and what exactly would be the purpose – to tell them how sad Oswald was? All of this was racing through his head as he walked out of the Mercury building.

The streets were noisy, and Andrew wished he was back in the country. He pulled his scarf up higher, trying to block out the sounds. Yet somewhere in the distance, he could hear what sounded like a radio station. He stopped for a moment and lowered his scarf – nothing but street commotion, and then it started to rain. Stepping into a shop doorway for shelter, he pulled up his scarf once more. Then again, he could hear a radio in his mind. It sounded like a debate. Several people were speaking, often at the same time, and he tuned into the dialogue. The subject was around whether the living could communicate with the dead. Laughter was heard at the mention of Ouija boards and holding a séance – and he began to imagine that these were demons from the other side.

Andrew called out in a firm voice. "I'm listening."

A passer-by gave him a strange look. There was a silence within him as he held his breath, which was broken by a car horn. More clearly than before, Andrew heard the words.

"Someone has broken through. Did you hear that? Is anybody there? What is your name? What do you want of us?"

Being asked such basic questions, he could not withhold himself. "My name is Andrew Harker. I am a journalist in Leeds, and I'm looking for the truth."

Radio interference screeched through his head, and he instinctively moved as if to regain a signal. Nothing, all was lost. The cold seemed to be eating down to his bones as he stepped back onto the pavement. His one intention was to get home, put the fire on and have some soup.

The bus was waiting as he entered the station, which was strange as it was only twenty past the hour. Darkness had fallen quickly, and he could see nothing but blurry lights through the window. The journey seemed slow, not being able to see where he was. Eventually, the bus stopped, and there was a pause.

"Your stop, mate," the bus driver shouted.

Andrew was the sole passenger and so did as he was told. As the bus pulled away, he remained for a moment under the shelter. He was confused – he was not where he expected to be. There was nothing familiar around him. He turned automatically to the left and took the next right. The sky cleared, and a full moon shone down the street where he lived. Home at last. Andrew lit the stove for heat and some soup. He was sure that once he had some food inside him, he would feel much better. Andrew sat back in the chair and drank the last of his soup. He looked long into the empty cup, feeling he needed to sleep.

"Is anybody there?" The words seemed to come from the bottom of the cup.

"Yes," Andrew said, speaking into the cup. "It's me again. Andrew Harker. I need to know the truth." There was a long pause.

"We can hear you, Andrew. Thank you for calling out to us. How can we help you find peace?"

Andrew sighed. "I never believed in ghosts, but now I know they exist. I need to write more about Oswald – perhaps there is a family out there who need to know how much he cared for them."

Andrew's head buzzed briefly, then faded to nothing. All was lost. He threw the cup across the room, and it smashed against the wall, followed by empty silence.

Susan heard the screech of brakes, a bang, and then quiet as traffic came to a standstill. She ran to the archive window where she could see a man lying motionless in the road – it was Andrew.

The Mercury reported the next day, in one of their minor columns, how a talented and successful reporter was tragically killed in a collision with a motor vehicle. He would be greatly missed by his colleagues as a man in pursuit of truth.

The Mystery of Ebbe House

Preface – If you didn't know what you were looking for, how would you know if you found it? The truth is that most of the time, we find things we are not looking for and, strangely, at a time when it is most needed. If we had learned this principle in our childhood, we might have saved ourselves a lot of time, stress, and worry. Invariably, life does not work out the way we would like it to. Most of the time, it seems like life itself is just trying to mess things up for us, creating emotional turmoil – often because we are not getting what we expect or what we want.

Opening – Our story begins on a most ordinary kind of day when the least expected incident occurs and throws Luke onto a trail of discovery. It was a Friday teatime when the phone rang. Great Uncle Robert, who had been ill for a while, had taken a turn for the worse. Luke's father was Robert's only living relative. The call from the nursing home was for them to go to Inverness,

Scotland, at once. This was not a trip for a twelve-year-old boy, so arrangements were quickly made to drop Luke off at his uncle Harry's. There was such a rush to pack essentials and to set off on their long journey from the seaside town of Whitby.

Luke tried to object, saying he could easily stay with a friend, but his parents, particularly his mother, were insistent that this was the best way. Harry was Luke's mother's eldest brother, and having never married, he lived on his own at Ebbe House, a large, dusty old house which belonged to Luke's grandparents. Visits to Uncle Harry's were infrequent. He came across as a grumpy person, and Luke did not look forward to his stay. He kept asking his parents, how long will this take, and will I be back at school on Monday? We don't know, was the only answer.

Arrival – Uncle Harry's house was perched on a cliff overlooking the sea, close to St Abbs, Berwickshire. The building had long fallen into disrepair, as Harry was lacking in funds. His sister would say it was no wonder as he had never had a proper job. Harry had great dreams of becoming a writer and publishing a best seller. The reality was that he barely earned enough to live on, writing as a freelance journalist. The car slowed as it turned into the long drive up to the house, and Dad steered as best he could as the car bumped over the potholes. Arriving, Mum banged on the front door. It seemed forever till the door opened, and there stood Uncle Harry. He asked them to come in, but Luke's parents insisted they leave straight away. It was still a long drive up to

Inverness. Luke was stood on the doorstep with his big overcoat, haversack and sleeping bag.

"Well, come in, lad, don't just stand in the doorway. The fire is on in the study."

Light bulbs were missing all over the house, casting shadows over the artistic plasterwork on the walls and ceilings. There was barely enough light to see where you were going. The lack of colour created an impression of an old-fashioned movie, which could easily have been a horror. Luke shivered, for it was cold, too. He thought that things would surely look better in the morning when the sunlight came in through the windows.

"Throw your things over there," Uncle Harry said. "I will show you to your room later. I expect you are hungry. What do children eat for supper these days? I have never married, never had children – far too busy for that sort of thing. My life is in books. One day, I will write a best-seller, and then this will become a beautiful mansion, restored to its original grandeur." Uncle Harry didn't wait for a reply but went to the kitchen. Luke could hear pots clanging and Harry chattering away to himself.

There was no other way to describe the room and, for that matter, the rest of the house – what he had seen of it. It was an utter tip. Luke had to move a pile of old newspapers to be able to sit down. He took off his glasses and wiped them, though it made no difference to what he could see. So, this is what happens when there are no parents to keep us in check. Uncle Harry had been left to run wild with his dreams. Luke could hear his mother's words echoing in his head. He only sat for two seconds before he was back on his feet and stepped into the pool of light, which was Uncle Harry's writing desk with a swivel wooden armchair in front of it that screeched as it turned. He was afraid his uncle would come to see what he was doing. On the desk, Luke had noticed many weirdly scribbled symbols, like code or some strange mathematics.

"Here we go then," Uncle Harry said. "My favourite, beans on toast with an egg on top. I get the eggs from the farm along the road. The beans are from the supermarket, of course. Now, would you like tea or orange juice? I don't have any of that fizzy stuff, but we can go to the shops tomorrow."

Luke said he was happy with orange and sensed that his uncle Harry was trying to make him feel at home. The beans were piping hot, and Luke needed to blow on them, taking frequent sips of juice.

"We can have eggy bread for breakfast with bacon, and I have plenty of beans."

Luke scratched his head, "What's eggy bread, Uncle Harry?"

"Now, just call me Harry. It's less formal and saves on word count." He gave a nervous chuckle. "Eggy bread is what posh people call French toast. It's a slice of bread dipped in a beaten egg and then fried in a pan. I get the eggs from the farm down the road."

Luke noticed how Harry repeated the bit about the farm. Was he uneasy about having a young boy to stay? Mum said he had very few visitors and could be difficult to get on with. Anyway, Luke thought baked beans on toast was a good start to this unexpected adventure.

Harry's introduction (the mystery) – "My grandfather George built this house, which then passed to my father. Your mum and the rest of us grew up here. Grandad died when I was seven years old, but I remember him well – we were close. He always said there were secrets hidden in the walls and ceilings, which will lead you to treasure." Luke noticed Harry had an odd habit. His right thumb would rest under his nose while the forefinger gently stroked down the top of his nose. It almost looked like he was sucking his thumb.

The wind outside came whistling through gaps in the window frames, and the whole house seemed to creak and groan like an old ship at sea. The extensive wall creations were of a nautical theme, vessels upon large waves and dark clouds, the sort of thing you might see in a stately home.

As if Harry was reading Luke's mind, he began, "The house has many sounds. If you listen carefully, it talks to you. There are secrets to be found."

By now, Luke was convinced that Harry was a little crazy and quite eccentric due to being on his own for so long, surrounded by so many sights and sounds, which compelled him to chase the mystery.

"Your mum and I would often run around the house, looking for unusual items, symbols, or patterns. The problem with that, of course, is that there are so many of them. Grandad was quite artistic and over the top. We eventually gave up and decided it was just a tall story, a way to keep us occupied when it was too wet to go outside.

Grandad would say it's a mystery and there for anyone to find. If we asked our parents about the mystery, they would claim to know nothing – apart from the house and its secrets, which were memories for another generation."

Luke had been listening intently to Harry's every word. "I think there is treasure," Luke said. "And your grandfather wanted you to find it. He wouldn't want to spoil things, though, by telling you any more or showing clues."

Harry jumped up. "You see, that's what I have always thought. I have spent my life examining the walls in every room of this house. I made notes, too – though they make little sense to me now – like a jigsaw puzzle without a picture."

Luke stood up too and declared, "We could look together and read through your notes. We have all weekend to find the treasure, and it will be great fun solving the mystery."

Harry's face dropped. "I have spent so many years searching. It has almost driven me mad, but yours are new eyes, Luke, new eyes. You might be able to see what I can't. Maybe you are the generation that's going to find the treasure."

"Where shall we start, Harry? Do we work from the top of the house down or work our way up?"

Harry put the kettle on for hot chocolate, his right finger pointing towards Luke, who was trembling. "What we need is a good night's sleep and breakfast, then we can start. But that's the problem, you see. I don't know where to start. I have gone round this so many times." He was visibly upset, and Luke felt uncomfortable.

"In quiz games," Luke said, "the first question is usually the easiest to get you started. I am sure your grandad would have known that. Often, clues are numbered one, two, three or lettered a, b, c. We just need to find a sequence."

Shortly after that, Luke's phone pinged. It was a text from his mum.
Hi Luke. how are you? hope you are not being any trouble for Uncle Harry.
I'm fine mum. it's a cold old house but i have hot chocolate. we are GOING HUNTING for grandad's treasure tomorrow.
oh no. that's not a good idea. you should keep away from that nonsense. why not go for a nice long walk. Uncle Harry enjoys walking.
That would be boring and it's cold out there. we can have fun in the house. Uncle Harry is excited.
that's what i was worried about. it will all come to nothing, and you will both be disappointed.
i have to go mum. speak to you tomorrow.

Luke's bedroom looked out over the bay and beyond to the rocky lighthouse that beamed out in a constant ten-second cycle. There was still a howling wind out there, and the roar of the waves cut through. How was he to sleep tonight, what with the house groaning too? Strangely enough, the sounds became something of a lullaby, and before long, tucked up with a hot water bottle, Luke was fast asleep. There were dreams that night, processing all that had happened that most unexpected of days. Though he was not to remember any of them.

During breakfast, the treasure hunters began to talk about the unusual ways a treasure trail may be laid out.

"We must find the beginning, the first clue," Harry said. "I have spent years looking for things out of the ordinary in hopes of stumbling on the clues. Trying to see if there was a theme in Grandad's artwork. Secret panels or hidden drawers. I started to think it was all just a hoax, one of Grandad's tall stories."

One of Seven – There in the kitchen, upon the ceiling, was a written statement. "Once upon a time, there were seven seals," Luke shouted. "Once, the word one. Is that the first clue? Can we climb up and look closer."

There were lumps of plaster fashioned to look like rocks. On the smooth ceiling were painted grey seals, and yes, seven of them. The painting displayed the evening sun, low on the horizon, just above the kitchen window. The sunlight seemed to glisten off the backs of the seals, laying happily on the rocks. A reassuring, peaceful image for what would have been a busy kitchen. Luke, by now, was standing on tiptoes in the corner near the sink, peering hard at the rocks speckled with tiny holes. Then, he spotted a larger hole. "Do you have a torch, Harry? I think there's something in here."

"Wait, let me climb up there," Harry said. "I'm taller. I'll bring my torch." The pair changed places and Harry confirmed, "There's something in here all right. I think there are some tweezers in the second drawer, can you pass them."

"Here you go." Luke held his breath while Harry poked around in the hole. Gingerly, it began to appear between the pincers. A rolled-up piece of paper, and as it came into full view, they spotted a red wax seal marked with a 1. Harry, not as young as he used to be, took his time getting down and then headed to the kitchen table. Using the tweezers, he carefully unpicked the seal and rolled out the paper.

Congratulations on finding the first part of my story. I wonder how long it took you. Seals were an important part of my life, spending time out on the cliffs, watching passing ships and listening to the sound of the seals. The colony sings together in long, slow, and mournful tones, creating a piece of beautiful music. This sound could hold me fast for quite some time and a love of the sea grew. I became a wickie, keeper of the local lighthouse – maintaining the clockwork lens mechanism, oil for the lamps and trimming the wicks. It was a lonely job, but I loved it out there. On a clear night, you can see for miles. Now, what else might you find at a lighthouse? Now you have started, don't give up. Satisfactory completion is always rewarded.

The pair of them were astounded. "I knew it," Harry said. "I knew it was true. The whole story must be here, now we have found number 1." Harry's feet were dancing with excitement, like a young boy at Christmas time.

Two of Seven – "I bet there are seven parts to this story," Luke said, "leading us to the treasure. Once upon a time, there were seven seals. My bedroom has a picture of a lighthouse."

And off they went, up the stairs. Young Luke took two steps at a time and arrived first. They stood there in the quiet for what seemed like an age, staring at the wall with the window in the middle. Yes, there was the lighthouse embedded in the cliff. Unmovable, dependent and pushing its light out to sea. But what else might we find at a lighthouse?

"I see it," Harry shouted. "Are they wooden barrels, barrels of oil for the lamp? Look closely around where they are standing."

And sure enough, another hole like the first one, and out came the tweezers. "This one is stuck. I don't want to tear it or damage the plaster." Harry gently scraped away a little plaster around the hole. It was full of dust and grime from over the years. "I've got it," Harry said. "Let's go to the window to read what we have." The number 2 seal was opened, and Harry placed his hand on Luke's shoulder. "Come on, lad, you read this one."

At that moment, Luke's phone pinged again. "I'd best answer, it's Mum."

hi Luke. how are you today?

Having fun. we have found two messages from your grandad hidden in the walls. he was a lighthouse keeper. we are going to find the treasure.

why can't you just do as you are told? stop that nonsense. do something else instead. i don't want Uncle Harry filling your head with rubbish. we are picking you up tomorrow and that will be an end to it.

okay mum. talk to you later.

Luke returned to where he was, giving Harry

a knowing smile. "Mum's fine, just fussing."

"Okay, so long as she is fine. Read on, lad."

Foul conditions could blow in fast and whether you could see vessels out there or not, the light in the darkness should never go out. A big responsibility, for lives may be in peril and seamen depend on the light, keeping them away from the rocks. There can be signs of madness in this solitary task, now attributed to the mercury used to float the lens with ease in its turning. Learning the necessary skills was not difficult – it was keeping it all in peak condition, along with my mind. Fear and demons were frequent, what if this were to happen? What if that? When I am most needed, will I be ready? All parts work together, but the part that holds the flame is the wick.

Three of Seven – "Out of this bedroom," Harry said, "turn left, and down the corridor, there is a tiny room. We have only ever used it for storage. In there, the wall is decorated as if it were a workshop. There are lots of disassembled parts on a bench. We used to call it Grandad's workshop."

As if they were racing against the clock, both headed quickly in that direction. It was necessary to move an old bed frame and a chest of drawers to give a full view of the wall and its collection of parts. Mostly, items were painted on the wall and sitting on a wooden beam, which was the workbench. Luke and Harry studied the items in silence. A partial lens, a barrel of oil, a telescope, and a multitude of other parts they could not name. In the corner and resting on the bench top was a box. Not a painting, a real wooden box.

Luke tried to open the lid, but it didn't want to move.

"Harry, can you try and lift it."

Harry moved in and took a closer look. The slight gaps in the box pointed to it being a drawer, not a box. This was still tight and looked as if it had not been opened since the day it was made. Harry used his pocket knife to tease it open and found six miniature wicks in their holders. Down the centre of one wick was a now familiar scroll with a red seal marked 3. "Your turn to read this one, Harry."

Well done for getting this far. I wonder what year it is now you are reading this. I was in my thirtieth year, with quite some experience of lighthouse keeping. There were set ways of doing everything, ensuring the continuity of directed light. It can't be expressed enough just how life-saving the light is. Light will always penetrate the darkness. However, some elements can affect the light. It was one such night that same year, when all that could go wrong, battled to extinguish the light. There was no way of knowing if there were vessels in the area. Could I hold it together through the height of the storm? Come and relive that storm with me.

Four of Seven – After a stunned silence, Harry was the first to speak. "It must be the storm room at the back of the house." They both rushed downstairs towards the rear lounge. The clock in the hall struck noon. Almost three hours had passed since breakfast, but it seemed much shorter than that. Harry and Luke stood side by side on the threshold of the storm room.

Something prevented them from stepping inside. The decoration in this room extended to all four walls. It was both beautiful and fearful.

"As children, we rarely came in this room," Harry said. "Dad would sit in here on his own, for some peace and quiet, he would say." Luke took one step forward and began to look around the room. Harry continued. "I think we need to move all the furniture into the middle of the room. That way, we can see everything." They set to, pushing and dragging items over the wooden floor. The weather outside contrasted with the storm scene, so Harry had the thought to close the internal window shutters and put on as many lights as he could find.

"Now then, Luke, I think we have earned a cup of tea and a sandwich. What do you say?" Without waiting for an answer, Harry added, "There's a book of my dad's I want to find, too. You put the kettle on, and I'll be back from my study in a flash."

Luke would have rather pushed forward in the storm room, but the thoughts of a cup of tea and maybe ginger biscuits proved the stronger option.

Harry returned carrying a book. "Here we are. I read this book a good few years ago, it's the story of the Eyemouth disaster, just along the coast here. It happened in 1881. Grandad was born in 1880, but his father may have known folk involved." Sat at the kitchen table, Harry continued. "The sea was calm, though a storm was forecast on what was to be called black Friday. Fishermen in their boats left the harbour. Their livelihood depended upon what the sea would give them. A ferocious storm rose, boats were overturned, and many dashed against the mainland rocks. One hundred and eighty-nine men were lost that day."

After a sombre moment and finishing their snack, Harry and Luke returned to the storm room in silence. They sat in the middle among the furniture, trying to take in the full force of the imagery. Some of the clouds were backlit by lightning flashes. This could easily be a 360° view from the top of the lighthouse.

"Where do we start looking for seal 4?" Luke asked. "It could be anywhere."

Harry scratched his chin. "People talk about the eye of the storm, around which everything circles – there can be a stillness there."

Two pairs of eyes scanned the full room, looking for a pattern and a place of stillness. Everything looked merciless – how you might imagine the end of the world.

"There, on the ceiling," Luke shouted. "That group of clouds circling."

"You might be right. Let's go and find a ladder. I had best do the climbing. It's a long way up there."

With the ladder safely against the wall, Harry ascended step by step. Luke did as he was asked and kept his foot on the bottom rung. He couldn't imagine how that would help should the ladder slip. The top of Harry's head brushed the ceiling, and he peered into the cluster of clouds. A small hole had been drilled into the plasterboard, and out came the tweezers. After some scraping around, the scroll of paper was brought into the light. "Yes. number 4." Harry came slowly down, and they sat in the middle of a large settee. "Do you want to read this one, Luke? It's your turn."

Luke shook his head. "No. It's too scary. You read it."

I wonder who you are, sons, daughters, grandchildren, some distant generation. Or even strangers, picking over the old house. You have arrived at seal number four – good luck.

My name is George Benfield, born in 1880. At the age of twenty-three, I became a lighthouse keeper, or a Wickie as we used to be called. Our task was to keep the wick trimmed, the lamp burning and the heavy lens turning. A lonely job out on the jagged coastline of St Abbs.

It is often said that there is an eerie calm before a storm, I can vouch for that. Now, we never know quite how dreadful things are going to be till we get there. So, there is no need to worry in advance, we must get on and do our job. When the storm first arrived, it was as if the wind and rain were trying their hardest to destroy all in its path. It was impossible to see if any vessels were coming close to the perilous rocks. Knowing the importance of the light was everything. The hours without sleep were pulling me in opposing directions, and I felt that I was losing my mind. Keeping the light burning throughout the storm must be my only thought.

Five of Seven – The story had taken the treasure hunters into the storm without significant detail of what happened that night – except the importance of holding the light. George's words did not seem to lead anywhere. How would they find number five?

"What about the last word…" Luke said. "Thought? Where in the house would you go to find your thoughts?"

"Well, what's a thought, and where does it come from? Sometimes, I need quiet. At other times, it just happens when I am busy doing something else." Harry was busy rubbing his nose again. "My study room is my thinking place."

"I go up into our attic room at home," Luke said. "It's where I find my best ideas."

"The smallest room in this house is like an attic. But it's more like a lighthouse, a lookout post – it faces the sea." Harry led the way. "It's on the first floor at the end of the corridor. You could mistake the entrance as being part of the wall panelling."

This sounded exciting, a secret door.

Luke's eyes widened. "Oh, a hidden staircase. Can I open the door?"

"It's not hidden, just not often used. Here we are."

The door sprung open to reveal a clockwise-turning staircase up and into a small room. Harry went up first, telling Luke to be careful and to hold onto the handrail. It was barely a room just a small wooden structure. Its window covered half the room's circumference and supplied more than enough light. Looking from the outside, it might be described as a turret.

Luke perched on a high stool facing the window. "This is an amazing place to sit, think and write, Harry."

"Oh no. I need my books around me, and I would be forever running up and down for cups of tea. No, this wouldn't work for me."

Harry was busy touching the walls and rafters, searching for scroll number five. Looking out of the window, Luke experienced a strange phenomenon. It was as if the whole room vanished, leaving him sat in mid-air, gazing out to sea. Luke shook his head and blinked two or three times. The window reappeared with him safely inside.

"It's the window, Harry. Gazing out of the window creates thoughts we didn't know we had. Check around the window frame."

They explored the frame with their fingers. Harry, being much taller, ran his fingers across the top of the lintel. There was an unnecessary bump. A small fishing boat had been carved into the lintel. Feeling a loose part on its deck, Harry took his pocket knife and prised it open. Sure enough, there was a scroll with seal number 5.

"You were right, young man. This one is for you to read. You're in the high seat."

Luke took the scroll, opened it, and read.

I am glad you could join me here in my little lighthouse. Although I did not remain a lighthouse keeper, the lighthouse never left me.

You will recall that we were in the storm. It had still not reached its peak, and my ability to keep going seemed to be fading. What if I just couldn't do it, and lives were lost? Thunder was a constant rumble and bangs. Lightning flew across the sky, leaving imprints of the black rocks in the backs of my eyes. I was terrified as I battled to keep the flame burning. It felt as if the windows would burst through at any moment. If that were to happen, all would be lost. I told myself that the lighthouse was well-built – but there were doubts.

At my lowest point, I stopped, and through the relentless noise of the storm, I could hear a voice. Not out there in the storm, but in the room. The outside storm seemed to quieten, and it was my father's voice I could hear. 'Hold fast, son, I'm with you.' There were now two of us carrying this load, and I was not going to give in. The storm cleared by morning light, and I was able to rest.

All my achievements, and the things I have made, I always felt I could do better. It took me a while to realise that our best at the time is always sufficient. In your search for number six, consider the word faithful.

Six of Seven – Harry scratched his face. "This is getting harder. Where do we go from here?" He had dreamed of these clues being found all his life, and the treasure, of course.

They were so close now. Young Luke remained fascinated by the outside view, waves crashing into the rocks – he could quite easily have stayed there all day. After a cursory discussion, the pair decided to break for lunch. It was almost three o'clock. Cheese sandwiches, pickles and crisps were laid on the table and both ate heartily.

Luke appeared deep in thought. "A penny for them," Harry said.

"I was thinking the last part was not really about the storm. It was your grandad's achievements and him not feeling good enough." He paused while he put his last pickled onion in his mouth, which made his eyes flicker as the vinegar hit the inside of his cheek. "If Grandad was standing back and looking at his creation –

the house, it would be from the outside."

After they had finished their meal, Harry agreed they should look, and they headed to the front door. Standing a fair distance from the house, they could see it in its entirety. It was a strange mix of gothic and traditional as if it had been built without a specific plan for how it would turn out. The turret did look like an afterthought. It was traditional in the sense that the door was in the middle, with windows on either side.

"Yes," Harry said. "The front looks like a face. The door is its mouth, everything comes and goes through the doorway. Let's go and have a closer look. Something about faithfulness?"

There was a burst of new energy as they hurried towards the doorway. There didn't seem to be anything special about it. No ornate carving, holes for hidden scrolls or painted images. But there was something, it was difficult to make out, though it looked like words on the edge of the door frame.

"You might be right, Luke. I'll go get a damp cloth." Harry returned and gently wiped down the woodwork. The words could only be read when standing edgeways to them, allowing the light to reveal the letters. It read: 'Looking down upon Methuselah. Faithful bonus.'

Harry touched the words with his fingertips. "There was a family dog that Grandad called Methuselah, who lived to a ripe old age, although his real name was Bosun. Only family members would know that. Thanks, Grandad. Love you."

Luke sensed the moment, though he had not experienced that kind of special relationship. That minute was interrupted by another text from Mum.

picking you up tomorrow around midday. Uncle Robert is getting better, a false alarm. what are you doing? mum.

reading stories about lighthouses, and how they have to keep the light on during the storm. i'll tell you all about it on our way home tomorrow.

that will be nice. sleep well. how's Uncle Harry.

he's good. happy and laughing. we've had a good day. can i come again soon.

we'll see. but that doesn't sound like Uncle Harry. see you tomorrow. sleep tight.

Luke sighed in relief – that went well. There was no mention of their quest. Mothers do not understand this kind of need. They just want to spoil everything. Now, where were we?

"Bonus is an anagram of Bosun," Luke blurted out.

"Yes, and he's buried in the shade of a tree to the left of the driveway, about fifty yards from here."

Seven of seven – Heading away from the house, the pair walked briskly towards Bosun's resting place. Surely, they were not meant to dig up poor old Bosun? The walk broke into a run as they shouted Whoop whoop! Then came the quiet, looking down at the overgrown grave, wondering what next… They were doing what was written, looking down upon Methuselah.

Luke turned and looked up at the tree. "It's the tree," he shouted. "The tree that's looking down over Methuselah. Could that be a hole in the tree? Look, up there – a hiding place."

"You might have something there, young Luke. Shall I lift you? I think you could reach that standing on my shoulders."

That sounded a little scary to Luke, but they had come this far, and they were too excited to waste time looking for a ladder. Harry pushed Luke up the tree trunk and then guided his feet, one to each shoulder.

He straightened up to his full height when Luke shouted, "I'm there. I can see into the hole."

"What can you see, lad? What's there?"

"Just leaves and dirt. I can't see anything."

"Put your hand in, clear out the rubbish. It must be there, whatever it is."

Luke pulled out leaves which rained down on Harry's head, and he started to splutter. "Sorry, Harry. Wait… I think there is something here. A box, a tin box, it's a tight fit."

"Grab it, lad. Let's have it down here and see the treasure."

The firmly closed and rusted box was around twelve inches by eight and about two inches deep. There was some weight in it. Being unsuccessful in prising the lid off, they opted for the kitchen and a can opener. The process was quite a ceremony, a real build to reveal the contents. Luke was just as excited as his uncle. However, the result was stunned silence, nothing shiny or sparkling – just an old notebook. Harry removed the book and gave it a shake, but nothing fell out. A quick flick through the pages gave no inclination to further steps, no map, and no conclusion. Harry turned to put the kettle on, though I am sure he would have welcomed something stronger. This was a real disappointment. Their hopes and dreams were finally dashed.

Meanwhile, Luke had been reading quietly. There were words of congratulations for uncovering the clues and finding the treasure. Also, written in the same hand, there was a complete set of clues and their hiding places. There were stories, too, as to how these clues came into being, and a back story to the building of the house.

Harry gave a long sigh. "Well, that's it. All for nothing, I should have known. Time wasting at its best."

Luke's eyes widened. "It's a book. It could be a best seller. You just need to finish and publish it in your grandad's name. Look, there are many more parts to the story yet to be found. It's a story that's meant to be shared forever, for many generations. That sounds like some treasure to me. Your best-seller, Harry."

Finale – Mum and Dad picked up Luke on Sunday afternoon as wind and rain blew in from the sea. Harry greeted them with a smile and a big hug for his sister and then waved them goodbye. It took Luke the whole journey home to tell the full story.

Harry settled into writing that same evening and began the story he entitled "The Mystery of Ebbe House." He found the rest of his grandad's artwork most helpful, as he could now see where it all fitted together. It took many months to write, edit and re-edit. The publishers thought the story would not be believed, and so categorised it as fiction. Finally, the manuscript was sent, and indeed, it was to become a best seller. Even Mum enjoyed reading it, eventually.

Uncle Robert made a partial recovery and went on to live another two years. Following this extraordinary weekend, Luke was determined to work hard at school. He would aim to progress through the Police Force to become a Detective Inspector. Whatever life would bring, Luke knew that if he only did his best, that would be sufficient.

JOHN PEARSON

The Man Behind the Nab (With the rhubarb slippers)

From my mum and dad's bedroom window, I could see Eston Nab and the beacon standing tall. The beacon was built in 1808 as a watchtower to warn of Napoleon's invasion. It was demolished in 1956, and a monument now stands in its place. From my home in South Bank, I would use this as a focal point for my new telescope.

School days brought exciting stories of SS Castle and Ghost Town, hidden paths, and tunnels. Often, with friends, we would walk to the Nab, then on to Roseberry Topping and Captain Cook's Monument. Nab is the name given to a rocky outcrop, but it conjures up more than just a windy ledge at the top of a hill. It was a place to escape to above the smog of the town. Historians say folk were living there back in 700 BC.

My dad would often come out with stories or just quirky phrases – strange and funny but leaving you with thoughts and questions. Dad said one day, "Have you heard of the man behind the Nab with rhubarb slippers?" Of course not, and I don't recall ever hearing anything since. This didn't stop me from wondering – there must be some truth in it because dads know everything.

The man behind the Nab sounds very much like a solitary figure, living out of reach of the town's folk below. We might refer to him as eccentric in his choice of garments and abode. Teased and made fun of, this man of no name would not want to venture from his choice of isolation – lost in the many descriptions of his nature.

I am imagining voices down in Eston Square: 'He's over six feet tall and has never cut his hair, living on berries and wild honey. I hear he talks to animals and trees – he's quite mad. The man can cast spells and, at night, turns into a hare. He has forgotten how to speak but can be heard screaming at the moon. His home cannot be seen, as it's covered by magic.' Blame would be placed at this man's feet for all manner of misfortune, sickness, or disaster.

Today, our man behind the Nab might be deemed an eco-warrior. It seems that those who make the most out of life, make the most out of what they have.

The Eston Hills brought forth iron ore, and those who came from many a mile created this 'Ironopolis' and all that was to follow. The iron ore has long gone, and much more besides. The people who remain are of good stock and remember the stories of old. However, there is darkness and despair as to the future.

Our choice now is still related to our man behind the Nab (with the rhubarb slippers). Is he to be ridiculed and blamed or modelled as an eco-warrior so that we might make the most out of what we have now?

Not to be disillusioned by how we see things now, but to realise one opportunity after another – by digging deep inside to find a different kind of ore. The word 'ore' incidentally, means rock containing minerals. A mineral is something of value, a natural substance of an ordered structure. Our mineral has never left the Cleveland district. It has been held in life stories and is ready to emerge again.

Our identity is not in what we do or how we do it. It is in the deep value of how we create one thing after another. And the strength is in doing it together.

The final ingredient is belief.

It's all in the Attic (You can always change your mind)

How wonderful would it be to have a guidebook to your mind and an instruction manual to enable peak performance, or at least to have a basic understanding? So, welcome to the attic – the keeper of memories, dreams, and imaginings – treasures and possessions, those that are stored, and some that are hidden. The attic is often little used, awkwardly shaped, and dusty. A space with exposed rafters and difficult-to-reach corners. Let us be clear from the outset, I am the attic – an allegory for your mind. There are ground rules for the would-be explorer.

Your attic is a space outside of time, with the capacity to hold eternity. It will never be empty, though it benefits from a little clearing from time to time. The rafters and supports give shape and form to your thoughts and provide a means of translation. There is infinitely more in every attic than you can imagine, and I invite you to exercise that imagination frequently.

You may say, there is nothing much in my attic, and that may be true in your version of reality. But we both know we are talking about something more than just a storage space and cast-aside items. This is a space where everything comes together and encompasses the entirety of your structure. You know how important that is.

Just think for a moment about how we create our memories (did you imagine they just happened)? This is the way we begin to make sense of the things we see, hear, and feel. Comparing each new experience to our memories – forming our beliefs of how things are.

Each attic is unique in its structure and contents, but there are so many similarities that you may be forgiven for thinking that we are all in the same attic. These attic rooms can remain a museum or become an engine room, driving us forward.

Another force lurks in the shadows, not always apparent and never clear as to its purpose. Often sensed but never seen, it can emerge at the most inopportune moments. If this force could be found, I recommend you lock it in a strong chest, for it can be destructive even in small measures. Take comfort in knowing that there is a guardian in the attic, which is governed by forces that have your safety first.

This space should be regarded as a living area, an integral part of your house, rather than a space for the non-living. It is not designed for aesthetics, this area has a practical function and the positioning of a chimney and plumbing for the floors below. There is a tightness in the sides where the roof meets the walls, barely accessible and perceived as a wasted space. Even here, there are things to discover if we take the time.

Captured moments dwell here: photographs, childhood toys and books, and are all part of our learning process along with sports equipment and items for hobbies often purchased with good intentions. We cannot recover the cost, so we keep them with a promise that we will start again one day. Old clothes with a close emotional feel to them no longer fit, but that emotional thread is too strong to break. All these items find their way to the attic. Things that we rarely use such as Christmas decorations and other oddments we do not want on display in the rest of the house.

What will we find in this attic of ours? Things collected, inherited, or perhaps you are only acting as a custodian. Things of value, financial or emotional, or perhaps you are holding something through superstition. "I had better not get rid of this or something will happen!"

Entering the attic can be a challenge. The hatch or door is often locked, and stairs to it must be assembled or let down – very few have direct access, and effort is required to achieve this ascent. A very different space lies within, and care should be taken, for it is easy to bump your head or trip over boxes often left around in no particular order.

Some attics have a permanent staircase, but there is usually a door at the top or the bottom. We look at that door or hatch, and fear rises as to what might be up there. A bolt or key secures our fear and holds the darkness at bay. A skylight or electricity would be a luxury. Mostly you would need to take your light – a torch, to chase the shadows as they stretch from the floor to the ceiling.

This is a separate room from the rest of our house and seems to be much smaller than the floor space below. We tend to make a noise as we enter as if to scare away anything we do not want to see. Everything is here, from beginning to end, and frequent visits will disturb the dust.

The attic contents will first have a visual impact, but I invite you also to listen and feel – use all your senses. Smaller things are often harder to find but can be quite significant, and they usually turn up when you are looking for something else. Be aware of distractions, they will consume your time in the attic and may discourage you from returning.

There is a methodology here in the attic, though it may be hard to see. The patterns emerging are formed by our experiences (memories). Take time to get to know them and rearrange them if you feel the need. Sailing in strange waters, we need to have a reference point and if we cannot see one, we should create one. Have you noticed how when we are in an unfamiliar place, we begin to see people who look like people we know? Placing a friendly reference in our unfamiliar space provides us with a sense of security.

Patterns flow through our very being. There is a structure in our DNA. Understanding this structure enables advancement in medical knowledge. Creating a model of our attic (even though it may be imaginary) enables understanding. From the moment we exist, we begin to replicate without thought or reason – most of these are quite helpful. We build patterns of behaviour – following others and accepting it as normal. Occasionally, a pattern or process may be revealed to be quite unhelpful. Just like a computer programme, we run the process repeatedly, oblivious to the operation or the underlying effect it is having. Wouldn't it be good to uncover these hidden programmes and begin to alter the process, bringing about better outcomes? All this is possible and should be encouraged. To neglect this activity is to be blown any which way the wind blows.

Stories are created in the attic, (we do it all the time), it helps us make sense of what is happening and how we feel. If we can put it in a story, then all is well in the attic. What kind of things keep happening that drive you crazy? This will give you a clue as to where to look. Change is always possible, but not always in the way you first imagined. Remember, the attic has your safety and best interest at heart.

Be bold in your uncovering, a little at a time. See the benefits and go on to do more. This is a process and has a pattern. Once the pattern is recognised, it becomes a friend.

It's good to have a very large sheet of paper in your attic – go ahead and create one now. This is for you to scribble down all the things you can imagine. Some will come from a prior experience or be prompted by sight, sound, touch, or smell. Once your thoughts are written on the sheet, you will find they can be placed in order, drawing out a plan of action and reaching your desired outcomes. This creates a sense of peace in the attic and encourages a productive working space.

Where does imagination reside? Nowhere and everywhere – in fact, it just appears, often when you least expect it. So, how might it be if you began to expect it?

An attic reflects towards us our unique construction of reality, we shape and form what we see, hear, and feel, creating stories around our experiences. Permit yourself to create how you want things to be – things that are equally good for you and for others. Clear space is necessary if you are going to move things around. You may think your attic is full, but all it needs is a little organisation, and you will see just how much space there is. I invite you to go to your attic often and stand with empty hands in that large space. It is a powerhouse of ideas and creativity waiting to be used. There is so much more you can achieve once you have accessed the attic and discovered its contents.

The Old Writing Desk

Auction rooms are fascinating places. You never know quite what is going to turn up. There is often a great buzz of people viewing the items – no one wishing to betray their interest. This particular day I had been quite taken with an old writing desk, the type that sits on a table. The desk had certainly seen better days, but I thought I might just put in a bid. As the auctioneer stepped up to the rostrum, the room fell into silence – the game was on. After almost half an hour of items sold and unsold, up came the writing desk.

"What am I bid," the auctioneer said. "£100 anywhere – 80, 60? Will someone start me at £40?" My hand flinched, then rose to my shoulder.

"Any advance on 40, 45 anywhere?" There was a long silence. The next thing I heard was, "Sold for £40. Number 215."

Arriving home, I found a space for my new acquisition on a small table in the living room bay window. Pulling up a chair, I opened the desk and took out ink, fountain pen and paper. There was also a domed glass paperweight that I hadn't noticed in the auction room, but I am sure it must have been there.

What to write, a letter, poem or a short story? As I enjoy a good yarn, I thought this would be an ideal choice. I stared out of the window for inspiration and then around the room. My head seemed quite empty. I looked again at the old writing desk, and that is what I wrote. 'The Old Writing Desk.' As the words appeared in deep blue ink, I noticed a reflection in the glass paperweight – it was the writing desk and someone sitting there writing, though it was not me. My pen left the paper, and the image faded. Look as I might, I could no longer see the reflection. Only when the pen again touched the paper could I see the gentleman at his desk. I tried to see how the reflection was arriving at the glass weight. It was independent of anything, apart from when the pen touched the paper.

I wrote how the gentleman was writing his memoirs and there came a swirling mist within the glass, clearing to reveal mountains and forest – my writer was an explorer. My hand moved quickly as I picked up the story, pausing only to refill the pen. Time seemed to stop as my character met wild beasts and hazardous paths through valleys and mountains. I dared not leave my seat, fearing losing the images – the source of my story. Or was it my story?

I had been captured and chained, held by a force not of this world, yet I had everything available to me to return to reality. The story was mysterious and seemed to be revealing something that had been hidden for almost a lifetime. Things that were beyond my understanding, but I was compelled to follow and do my part. Light was fading, and I found it difficult to see. I had to trust that this phenomenon would reappear when I returned.

The next day, I was not disappointed, and I soon completed the short story. Two or three stories further on, I became concerned that I was copying what I had been shown. I wanted to write my own stories, perhaps even get them published. From the window, I could see the pond at the bottom of the garden. Sunlight reflected in the water which flickered and danced. I used to tell my children there were fairies at the bottom of our garden.
Memories are my reflections and mixed with an element of imagination stories are created. I decided to put away the glass weight and allow my own words to appear.

Chasing Rainbows

It was a day like any other, with my regular walk across the fields and towards the moortop. My doctor recommended regular exercise, and I had to admit I did feel better for it. These walks became special moments, giving me time to do nothing but wander across the moor. It had looked like rain earlier, so I took my light coat with me. The weather here can be very changeable, and it pays to be prepared.

Light intermittently streamed through broken clouds as the gentle breeze shifted them across the sky. The earthy aroma of the moors mixed with the scent of sweet heather and oncoming rain. It's strange to think that we can smell rain before it arrives – something in our nose twitches, and it makes us shiver at the thought. I rested for a moment at the old boundary stone and decided this would be my turning point today. It was time to head back. Standing stones in these parts are often given names, and folk stories about them have been handed down through the generations.

This one is Old Jack, a shepherd out looking for his sheep. If you look from the eastern side, you can see his stooped posture and flat cap as he leans into the prevailing wind, his arm and right hand pressed into his pocket. Folk will say you can oft hear him whistle for his sheep.

I could hear the haunting sound of the curlew in the distance, with its complex harmonics and pitch variations. A bird often associated with the spirit world, usually a bad omen and referred to as the 'Seven Whistlers' – farmers would say it's going to rain. I, on the other hand, find their song uplifting and count it as a blessing to be heard. There was a mist drawing in, and rain was certainly on its way as I buttoned up my coat. I strode out and gauged that I would be back home before the rain.

The sun was behind me and cast a glow on the misty sheet in front. A pillar of light emerged that increased in intensity. Colours glowed in a rainbow sequence: red, orange, yellow, green, blue, and violet. Not a full bow, but a tall pillar I had never seen the like of. The colours seemed to seep into the ground, then in the blink of an eye – it could be seen as colours rising out of the ground and up to the heavens. The strange thing about this phenomenon was that as I walked towards it, it became closer – not what you would expect of a rainbow. Perhaps I'll find the crock of gold.

Before I knew where I was, the rainbow surrounded me. The colour of red drew out passion. I could feel the intense emotions of both love and hate – inevitably, love conquers hate. There was an urge to go and achieve what was right, as this red glow provided warmth, security, and the desire we needed to exist, stirring the embers of our core elements. There was a gradual change from red to orange to yellow, the colours of fire, fallen leaves, sunsets, and sunrise. Life inspiring in creation and rebirth through happiness, enthusiasm, and energy.

Yellows fade to green, immersing me in the reality of nature, a sign of new beginnings, a continuity of life and the things that live long after my brief time on earth. Countless shades of green are the most accepted though an unappreciated colour. Green transformed into the aura of blue, which quickened my heart. A freshness in the air that I could breathe and a thirst for cool, clear water. There was a sense of becoming part of the sky, rising above everything, and having a view of greater distance. This was a spiritual moment, as the deep violet carried me even higher still. There was nothing I could do and nothing I wanted to but to rest in this moment. Such peace, which I had never experienced before, filled every part of me, and I felt complete, as if everything was as it should be.

Time was irrelevant. The whole event may have only taken a minute, but it conveyed more than a lifetime of wisdom. I was aware that something extraordinary had happened and that life would become quite different.

Arriving home, the place where I rest, I sat and pondered on the crock of gold that I did not see. That precious commodity gold is the contentment that comes with the knowledge that not all we want can we have. To recognise also, that we have abundant things yet to be revealed, and all that we have, we do not own and will only come to fulfilment when we give it away.

JOHN PEARSON

About the Author

A Yorkshire man tends to tell things the way they are, honest and plain talking. Conversely, when writing fiction, it's important to tell a good tale. There seems to be an art in combining the two. Something John continues to strive for. While serving a charitable company and working with teens and young adults. The opportunity to study psychotherapy was seized with both hands and used wisely. John could see a need that could not be met by one man and was determined to fill as many gaps as he could. One-to-one work with young people and time spent listening to their stories. John attempted to turn these stories around, showing that better outcomes were possible – many made significant changes.

All endings are just new beginnings, as John would often say. Also, those who made the most out of life – made the most out of what they had. (It pays to take time and see what you already have). John grew up with stories and listened well, for they still echo today. His strongest motivation is to enable change for those in need and who are willing to engage. If his writing has a genre, then it would be young adult fiction/ Self-help/Well-being. However, comments back from an older group have also been very reassuring. Life is a series of trials and errors. Hopefully, by learning from our mistakes and being encouraged by our successes, we can make progress. As we discover more about our inner self and purpose, we become more aware of the things that matter. We hope you enjoy John's stories. There's a lot of him in there. It would be great if you could uncover some Secrets of the Universe.

JOHN PEARSON

Other books by John

Brother David – A Long Journey Home

Timmy Flea – The Inner Circle

Thoughts & Words – That May Just Rhyme

Printed in Great Britain
by Amazon